IMAGINATIVE TALES

J.K. MILIKEN

Copyright © 2020 J.K. Miliken.

All rights reserved. No part of this book may be reproduced, stored, or transmitted by any means—whether auditory, graphic, mechanical, or electronic—without written permission of the author, except in the case of brief excerpts used in critical articles and reviews. Unauthorized reproduction of any part of this work is illegal and is punishable by law.

ISBN: 978-1-6847-1836-8 (sc)
ISBN: 978-1-6847-1835-1 (e)

Because of the dynamic nature of the Internet, any web addresses or links contained in this book may have changed since publication and may no longer be valid. The views expressed in this work are solely those of the author and do not necessarily reflect the views of the publisher, and the publisher hereby disclaims any responsibility for them.

Any people depicted in stock imagery provided by Getty Images are models, and such images are being used for illustrative purposes only. Certain stock imagery © Getty Images.

Lulu Publishing Services rev. date: 02/10/2020

Contents

Requiem for Adam Bardeen 1
The Lightning Warriors 7
A.L.O.H.A. 13
Green and Red Rocks 19
Writer's Block 27
Martian Mud Pie 29
Death's Apprentice 33
Mind Games 37
The Murder Witness 41
The Detective's Alter Ego 47
Last Stand Alaska 57
The Aftermath 69
The Gold Three-Head Chain 99
Scratch and Sniff 103
The Pearl of Andromeda 111
The Magical Mystical Detective Winterstorm 123
The Langston Twins Murder Mysteries 147

Requiem for Adam Bardeen

On APRIL 16, 2200, a Memory File Auditor named Adam Bardeen appeared in the lobby of Anamnesis Incorporated, requesting a meeting with its CEO, Allister Farley. The security officer took him directly to Stuart Crenshaw, Head of Security. The security officer knocked on his office door, and a voice beckoned them inside.

"Thank you, Mr. Jones, I'll take it from here," Stuart Crenshaw said.

The security officer returned to his post.

"Why are you here today, Mr. Bardeen?" he asked. "We're not scheduled for our annual audit until next month, which is usually done by Mr. Austin."

"Unfortunately, Mr. Austin will be undergoing a heart procedure, and he will not be able to do the audit at the scheduled time. If you like, you can call to reschedule," Mr. Bardeen said.

"That's not necessary," he said. "How many files do you have to audit today?"

"Let me look at my inventory sheet," Mr. Bardeen said.

He reached into his briefcase.

"How odd?" Mr. Bardeen suggested.

"What?" he asked.

"I only need to audit two files," Mr. Bardeen said.

"That is odd, isn't it?" he said. "It's usually between twenty and thirty files."

"The files are AF-01 and AF-02, and they've been red-flagged," Mr. Bardeen said.

Mr. Crenshaw brought File AF-01 onto the big screen. As they watched the memory, two men, which they couldn't identify, were lying on beds connected to a machine. When the process ended, the younger man executed the older man, but the memory repeated twice more.

"Has the file been damaged?" Mr. Bardeen asked.

"Let me check," he said.

Mr. Bardeen waited.

"The file shows different years of 2080, 2140, and 2200," he said.

"I think we better move on to the next file," Mr. Bardeen said.

After he opened File AF-02, they could see two men talking next to two men lying on gurneys.

"When are we going to kill Alexander Fleming?" the first man asked.

"I don't feel comfortable killing an unconscious man," the second man said.

"I don't either, but he paid us to do a job!" the first man said.

"He only paid us to prevent him from becoming the 57th President of the United States, not kill him," the second man said.

Suddenly, another man they couldn't clearly see nor hear appeared in the memory.

"Who the fuck are you?" the first man asked.

"I came here to stop you from taking Alexander Fleming's memories," he said.

The second man shot him.

"Who the hell was that?" the first man asked.

"No clue, but we're going to teach him a lesson," the second man said. "First, we'll extract Alexander Fleming's memories, reprogram them as specified, and then place them into John Miller after taking his memories. Second, we'll extract the dead man's memories, and put them into Alexander Fleming instead of John Miller's memories."

"How?" the first man asked.

"With this device," the second man said.

"Why did our employer pick John Miller to store Alexander Fleming's memories?" the first man asked.

"He has a history of depression and being on heavy doses of medication, which makes his brain susceptible to control and manipulation," the second man said.

The file ended.

"Do you remember your history, Mr. Stuart?" Mr. Bardeen asked. "The 57th President of the United States was John Miller, which was the time the Democratic Party had control over Congress. In 2081, they secretly funded a project for memory retrieval, storage, and cloning for those who could afford the service."

"Does that mean someone traveled back in time to change history?" he asked.

"It does, and whoever it was, hired those two men," Mr. Bardeen said.

"What about the dead man?" he asked.

"Not a clue, but now it's time to end my pretense," Mr. Bardeen said. "I know you don't remember, but we've had this same conversation a few times."

"I never met you until today," he said. "Wait…"

"The reason my employer sent me from the future is to prevent Allister Farley from cloning himself and others. Haven't you ever wondered why every CEO in your company had either been the father or the son with the same last name?" Mr. Bardeen asked. "But, after viewing those files, I must go back to 2079."

"Cloning? How?" he asked.

"In 2080, Mr. Farley cloned himself, but the process was challenging as his first three attempts failed, but then he did it. He told his employees that he was retiring as the CEO and that his son would take over. In the first file we reviewed, Mr. Farley killed his older self after his memories were retrieved and placed into his younger self. A few years later, he traveled back in time and stole his mother's ova, which guaranteed him several lifetimes. Since then, he's done the same for his elite clientele," Mr. Bardeen said.

"What are we going to do?" he asked.

"I'm sorry, but there is no we in this equation," Mr. Bardeen said.

He pulled out a weird-looking device.

"Thank you, Mr. Stuart, for helping me with the audit today," Mr. Bardeen said.

"I hope to work with you again, Mr. Bardeem," he said.

"Perhaps, we will, Mr. Stuart," Mr. Bardeen said.

After he left the building, Mr. Bardeen transported himself to 2079 just before Allister Farley first cloned himself. As he waited outside Mr. Farley's office building, he saw him coming up the sidewalk. As he bumped into him, he planted a tracker on him, hoping he would lead him to his hidden laboratory.

A few days later, Mr. Bardeem tracked Mr. Farley to a well-guarded building. He knew getting inside would be impossible, but what he did next was ingenious. He traveled back in time when the laboratory was being built and hid inside. When he exited the storage closet after moving forward in time, the laboratory appeared vacant. He set the timer on the mini-nuclear device to destroy the entire complex, but unexpectedly, someone shoved a gun into his back.

"Hello, Mr. Miller," Mr. Farley said.

"The name is Adam Bardeen!" he stated.

"How interesting," Mr. Farley said. "The men I sent to do a job didn't do as I asked, and they will pay dearly for their mistake."

"What are you talking about?" he asked.

"Your body once belonged to Alexander Fleming, and my men were supposed to put John Miller's memories into him, but instead, they used yours," Mr. Farley said. "May I ask, what you were planning to steal from my laboratory?"

"You have it all wrong, Mr. Farley," he said.

When Mr. Farley heard the click, his eyes grew wide.

The End

The Lightning Warriors

THE WAR IN Los Angeles began in July 2025 after the government declared martial law following the massive volcanic eruption at Yellowstone National Park. It was also the time when Malcolm Death tried to take control of the city by declaring war against the police department.

"All patched up, Officer Miles," the nurse said.

"Thank you," I replied.

As I hopped off the hospital gurney, Commander Marquez approached me.

"You need to come with me," he said.

"Where are we going?" I asked.

"There's something I need to show you," he responded.

We got into his police cruiser and drove to an abandoned warehouse. When we walked inside, we went to a storage room, where there were scores of AR15's and ammunition.

"So, the military finally came through for us," I said.

"It wasn't them," he said. "I found a note on my desk this morning telling me to pick you up at the mobile hospital at 2:00 pm and bring you here."

"How in the hell would they know where I'd be at 2:00 pm?" I asked.

"No clue, but you must have a guardian angel," he answered.

After several trips, we got everything moved to the Central Precinct, and from there, we distributed the ammo and guns.

A week later, we were fighting against Malcolm Death's Army in a torrential downpour, when several men appeared wearing some armor helped us win the battle. We had no idea who they were, but I assumed they were my guardian angels, and they vanished as quickly as they appeared.

For the next nine months, we won several battles because of them, but during our bloodiest one on June 10, 2026, they weren't around. I was angry because we lost nearly a hundred men that day, and I got shot again.

Two months later, as I walked home, I heard footsteps coming up from behind. As I began to walk faster, whoever they were, kept pace. As I was about to run, I was shot in the leg and hit the pavement. As I turned over, two men were standing over me.

"Time to die, Officer Miles," one man said.

"Fuck you," I said defiantly.

I expected to die when two shots rang out, but when I opened my eyes, both men were dead.

"Who are you?" I asked.

"Marcus Miles," he answered.

"That's my son's name," I said.

"I am your son," he stated.

"My son is only ten years old, and he lives with my ex-wife in Riverside, California," I said.

"I understand your disbelief because I'm not from your time," he said.

"Sorry, but I don't believe in science fiction, mumbo-jumbo," I said.

"Then how would I be here at this moment to save your life?" he asked.

"Maybe you've been following me," I replied.

"I'll concede that point," he said.

"Would helping me affect the timeline?" I asked sarcastically.

"Twenty-two years from now, an alien artifact is discovered in one of the ancient pyramids in Egypt. That artifact allows our scientists to actively view the past to find fixable deviations caused by evil people. They send my team into the past to fix those deviations, but we must remain below a one percent threshold," he said.

"Why one percent?" I asked.

"The artifact allows our scientists to see what would happen if certain events never occurred. The first attempt was to see what would happen if Adolph Hitler died before he came into power, but the outcome was unexpected when another man rose to power, shifting the outcome of World War 2 in favor of Nazi Germany. That was a five-percent deviation. After numerous attempts, they discovered that anything below a one-percent deviation wouldn't impact the timeline," he said.

"Is there any way to prove who you are?" I asked.

"A DNA test kit," he answered.

"Okay, but we need to get this bullet out of my leg first," I answered.

"Not to worry–I'm a trained medic," he assured me.

After we got inside my apartment, he removed the bullet like a pro, and then he sutured my leg. Afterward, he gave me some antibiotics from his time.

The next morning, my leg was back to normal. So, I got up and walked into the kitchen to make coffee, but it was already brewing. I sat at the small table with my mug in hand with the man, who says he's my son. That's when I saw the DNA test kit.

"Are you ready?" he asked.

"Let's get on with it," I said.

The test confirmed that he was my son.

"Now that I know who you are, what's next?" I asked.

"At the old Sweeney warehouse tonight, there will be a meeting for the leaders of Malcolm Death's army," he replied.

"And where would we get the proper attire?" I asked.

"While you were asleep, I got us the appropriate attire. The men who were wearing it no longer needs it," he answered.

"What's life like in the future?" I asked.

"Malcolm Death becomes a warlord over the western part of the United States because there was no one to stop him," he said.

"How is it possible to travel through time?" I asked.

"Our scientists discovered that lighting opens up a vortex into the past which the alien artifact can keep open for a few hours. That allows us to travel in time, and the reason we can only travel during thunderstorms," he said.

"That explains why you couldn't be here during our worst battle," I remarked. "It is possible to change the outcome of that battle?"

"No, because it would exceed the one-percent threshold," he answered.

"Then what would happen if we stop Malcolm Death?" I asked.

"That's the reason I'm here alone because ending him falls below the threshold," he said.

In the early evening hours, we walked into the warehouse wearing the attire my son obtained for us. When Malcolm Death came to the podium, he spoke before he introduced his second in command, and both of their voices sounded familiar.

"What time is their meeting tomorrow?" I whispered.

"At 7:45 pm," he whispered back.

When we returned to the warehouse the next night, I knew who those voices belonged. It was the two cops that I arrested for their crimes, but their attorney somehow got them off.

We killed the guards, and we went inside.

"Why are you here?" Malcolm Death yelled. "Can't you see that we are in the middle of an important meeting?"

We removed our masks.

"You're supposed to be dead, Officer Miles!" Hiller exclaimed.

"If I told you how I survived my assassins, you wouldn't believe me," I said. "So, I won't bore you with the details."

We gagged and tied them, and after we walked outside, we pretended to be the perimeter guards. When the other leaders went into the warehouse, we ran to a safe distance, and then Marcus pressed a button. We watched the warehouse turn into a giant fireball.

Two months later, as I sat at the kitchen table with my coffee, I realized that my son and I changed our futures, so I decided to call my ex-wife to work things out.

The End

A.L.O.H.A.

WILLIAM DAVENPORT JUST completed a government-contracted weapons project at Nano Technologies except for his project notes. As he looked at his watch, he was late for dinner and clocked out. When he got home, his wife, Bess, and Cody, his teenaged son, glared at him.

"Sorry, I'm late!" he said apologetically.

"You're always late, Dad, because you're too busy building death machines to keep your promises," Cody complained.

Cody went to his room and slammed the door.

"What promises?" he repeated.

"You promised him some father-son time today," she answered.

"I did, when?" he asked.

"What is so damned important that makes you late for dinner every night?" she asked.

"Not you, too?" he asked.

"Yes, me, too, because you're becoming a stranger to this family. We never see you when you leave, and you've been late coming home for several weeks, and to make matters worse, on weekends, you're downstairs working in your lab," she explained.

"The reason I've been working late is that I had to finish a government-contracted project, and let me remind you who supports this family," he said.

"If that's how you feel, you can sleep on the couch," she replied sadly.

She ran upstairs, crying.

At the crack of dawn, he was off to work again.

Since there were no new projects in the works, he left his job early to surprise his family. On the way home, he bought a gift for Bess and a video game for Cody, but when he got there, he found a note taped to the door.

Went to stay with my parents until you realize we're a family

He suddenly realized what his family meant to him, and he sat on the couch, feeling sad. After a while, he put a TV dinner into the microwave and fed the dog. Afterward, he went downstairs to his lab to work. As he reached for a glass beaker filled with hundreds of micro-bots, he accidentally knocked it onto the floor, where it shattered into a million pieces. He banged his fists on the counter because he had just lost several months of work. He went upstairs for the broom and dustpan, but when he returned, the beaker was on the floor intact. So, he chalked it up to him being tired.

The very next morning, he went downstairs to work on his thought-transference device and switched it on, but nothing happened. He then went upstairs to check on the dog when he heard a loud thunderclap. As he looked outside, he saw electricity dancing across a power line, which gave him an idea. He returned to his lab, ramped up the current on the device, and put it on his head. When he switched it on, the massive jolt of electricity knocked him unconscious, and he hit the floor with a thud.

As he awoke, someone was calling his name, but there wasn't anyone in the lab except for him. Then a voice said, "Look over here." He looked at the wavy lines on his monitor, but he still kept looking around.

"Where are you?" he asked.

"Right in front of you, Bill," the voice said.

"Wait, you mean?" he asked.

"Yes, you successfully copied your consciousness in here," the voice replied.

"What's it like in there?" he asked excitedly.

"The circuits feel like arteries, and the electricity, blood," the voice replied. "But we may have a problem. Government agents are looking over your recently completed project,"

"How would they know the project is complete since I add my project notes from here?" he asked. "Unless…"

"The house has bugs," the voice said.

"How do I find them?" he asked.

"Where's that old radio of yours?" the voice asked.

"Right!" he said. "But what should I call you?"

"Call me, Newt," the voice said.

Bill dug through several boxes in the garage, searching for the radio. After he found it, he replaced the old batteries, and then he turned it on to get a steady buzz. As he ran the radio across every wall inside the house, he found three bugs and then returned to the lab.

"How many bugs did you find?" Newt asked.

"Three," he answered. "But how did they get in my house?"

"Do you remember that unexpected Internet disruption a few weeks back and that strange man from the cable company appeared a few minutes later? I believe he's the one who planted them, but we now have a more serious issue. Those government agents are on their way here with termination orders," Newt said.

Bill quickly left the house and then parked up the street to observe. He saw three black SUVs pull into his driveway.

The government agents searched his house but found it empty. As they walked out, one of them shot the dog. When Bill returned home, he took the dog to his lab per Newt's instructions.

"Place the thought-transference device onto the dog because you're going to retrieve his consciousness," Newt explained.

A few moments later, the dog was barking inside the monitor.

"Next, get a blood sample, and inject it into the beaker with the micro-bots," Newt said.

As he watched, the blood vanished.

"Where did it go?" he asked.

"The micro-bots are analyzing it," Newt replied. "Now, pour the beaker on top of the dog."

The micro-bots rebuilt the dog in less than an hour.

"Now place the thought-transference device back onto the dog," Newt instructed.

The dog suddenly jumped off the table as though nothing had happened.

"I was designing the micro-bots to repair damaged human tissue on burn patients, but how did they rebuild an entire lifeform?" he asked.

"You were nearly there, but I kept doing the research," Newt said. "But now, there's a more serious problem afoot. Those government agents are on their way to terminate Bess and Cody, and anyone else in the house!"

Bill ran upstairs to call Bess, which took some convincing, but finally, she, Cody, and her parents left the house.

As Bess and Cody headed to her sister's house, three black SUVs appeared behind her. As she turned right, they stayed with her. She told Cody to call his father.

"What's wrong, Cody?" he asked.

"Someone is following us," Cody said.

"Tell your mom to lose them," he said.

Bess made a sudden turn into a parking garage, and drove to the top, and then down the long spiral exit. For a moment, she had lost them, but then they appeared behind her again. She then sped toward the freeway ramp, but one of the SUVs T-boned her car, causing it to flip into the air. After it crashed and rolled, one of the agents made sure they were dead.

"I'm sorry, those government agents just terminated Bess and Cody, but you can still save them," Newt said.

Bill pulled Bess and Cody from the wreckage before the police arrived, and then drove home. A few hours later, Bess and Cody were alive.

"How can we be alive?" Bess asked.

"Newt will explain," he answered.

"Who's Newt?" Cody asked.

"That would be me, Cody," Newt replied.

"You sound like my dad!" Cody exclaimed.

"I am a copy of his consciousness," Newt explained. "Sorry to interrupt the family reunion, but those government agents are returning here!"

"How much time do we have?" he asked.

"About twenty minutes," Newt replied.

He put the thought-transference device on his head to copy his consciousness again.

"What are you going to do, Dad?" Cody asked.

"When I go upstairs, lock the door to shield you from the blasts," he replied.

"But you'll be killed," Bess protested.

"While I'm upstairs, Newt will explain what you need to do," he said.

Bill quickly made two bombs from the C-4 he uses in his experiments and poured acetone throughout the house. He then made a double dead man's switch connecting the two devices. Before he sat down in his big Lazy-Boy chair, he poured himself a glass of Irish whiskey and sipped on it while he waited for the agents to appear. A few minutes later, seven men and one woman walked inside the house.

"So, you're the assholes who killed my dog and family!" he growled. "Why?"

"Because you're a national security risk," the woman said.

"Just because I built a weapon for the government?" he asked.

"We're just following orders, so it's nothing personal!" she answered.

"So, it wouldn't be personal if I let go of this?" he asked.

When the first bomb exploded, only Bill and one agent died. The other agents laughed. Then the second bomb exploded, igniting the acetone just as Bill planned. The flash fire quickly swept through the house, catching the other agents on fire, and they died screaming.

While their house burned, Bess and Cody retrieved Bill's body. Afterward, Bill set explosives inside his lab while the fire department kept the house fire from spreading to the other houses. Newt left the lab via the internet as Bill, Bess, Cody, and the dog through a secret tunnel that Bill built just in case of an emergency. The lab exploded, and the tunnel collapsed.

Eight bodies were found inside the house after the fire was out.

Later, there was a massive explosion at Nano Technologies, destroying the entire facility.

A month later, the Milton family moved into an empty house in Hawaii. After their furniture was delivered, Dr. Milton went downstairs to his new laboratory.

"Are you there, Newt?" Dr. Milton asked.

"Yes, I am here," Newt replied.

"Thank you for our new identities, new home, and money, but how did you do it?" he asked.

"I obtained your identities through the U.S. Marshal's Service because they think you're in the Witness Protection Program. The dead agents paid for your house and the money in your bank account from their offshore bank accounts," Newt said.

"I do have one question, Newt," he asked. "How long will we live?"

"I would estimate several hundred years because all of you are Advanced Living Organisms of Humanoid Adaptation, or what I call A.L.O.H.A.," Newt said.

They both laughed at the pun.

"That's fantastic! That gives me time to reconnect with my family," he stated.

The End

Green and Red Rocks

Aftᴇʀ ᴛʜᴇ Baʀɴaʙy Space Station activated their emergency distress beacon, their last message was something about green and red rocks, and then silence.

The very next day, the Barnaby Control Center in Miami, Florida, contacted NASA.

Two days later, retired Colonel Jerod Cooper, a NASA representative, met with Richard Barnaby and his Control Center Supervisor, Daniel Reeves.

"Have you reestablished contact with your station?" Colonel Cooper asked.

"We haven't as of yet," Mr. Reeves answered.

"What is your plan to rescue your crew?" he asked.

"There is no plan because both shuttles are docked at the station," Mr. Barnaby replied.

"Your crew has the means to leave, but haven't?" he asked bluntly.

"That's why I requested NASA's help," Mr. Barnaby said.

"I'm sorry, but NASA isn't authorized to launch rescue missions for civilian-run space programs," he stated.

"If it were possible, would you lead the mission?" Mr. Barnaby asked.

"If you could manage such a miracle," he replied.

Mr. Barnaby called his friend Mark.

"Hi, Mark, it's Richard," he said.

"How's the meeting going?" Mark asked.

"They're rolling out the usual governmental red tape," Richard said.

"Who did they send?" Mark asked.

"Colonel Cooper, and he's agreed to lead the mission," Richard explained.

"Let me make a call," Mark responded.

A few minutes later, Colonel Cooper's phone rang. NASA told him that a mission to rescue the crew of the Barnaby Station was a go.

"I don't know how, but the mission is a go," he said. "But, who were you speaking to on the other end of the line."

"A college buddy named Mark Braithwaite," Mr. Barnaby answered.

"You know the president?" he asked.

"For the past forty-five years," Mr. Barnaby said. "Before we leave for NASA, I want to ensure that Mr. Reeves will be the one running the ground operation."

"I think I can arrange it," he assured him.

Two days later, a twelve-member rescue team consisting of Colonel Cooper, Mr. Barnaby, and ten Navy Seals were on their way to the space station.

Three days later, they docked at the station. The crew gave no reply as they attempted to contact them, and they had to override the airlock mechanism.

As soon as they walked inside the space station, they found two dead crew members. When they rolled them over, they had a mummy-like appearance with two large puncture wounds in their chest. They then continued to the control room.

"Hold up," he said. "I thought I saw something moving."

He called out, but no one replied.

"Jacoby, Watkins, check it out," he said.

After they disappeared, there was gunfire and screaming. The colonel saw Jacoby running back with four strange creatures behind him.

"Inside the infirmary!" he ordered.

Jacoby barely made it.

"What kind of experiments were your crew conducting up here?" he asked.

"Nothing like that, I assure you!" Mr. Barnaby said.

"Jacoby, what happened to Watkins?" he asked.

"Those creatures caught us by surprise, and one of them pinned him to the ground, and sank its fangs into his chest. That's when I hightailed it back here," Jacoby explained.

A strange tapping noise was coming from inside a cabinet, and the colonel went to investigate. As he opened the door, a small creature ran out, and they shot it. When the colonel looked inside the cabinet, there were green and red rocks, and one of them was open.

"Those green and red rocks aren't what they appear–they're eggs," he said.

"Eggs?" Mr. Barnaby repeated. "Where did they come from?"

"My guess is from outside the space station," he said.

"And now everyone is dead," Mr. Barnaby lamented.

"We need to proceed to the control center, so let's line up to the left and right of the door, and prepare to fire," he ordered.

As he opened the door, two creatures ran in, and they shot them.

"Where are the other two?" Mr. Barnaby asked.

"Waiting for us outside!" he replied.

As they walked out of the infirmary, there was no sign of them. Suddenly, one of them grabbed a team member from above, and they shot both creatures.

"They must be able to communicate," the colonel said.

"Are you saying they're intelligent," Mr. Barnaby stated.

"Yes, Mr. Barnaby, that's what I'm saying," he answered.

They safely arrived at the control center without running into any more creatures.

"Mr. Barnaby, do you know how to operate the controls?" he asked.

"Of course, I designed them," Mr. Barnaby stated.

He did a room by room sweep to find his entire crew dead.

"I've known those men for years," Mr. Barnaby said sadly.

"I'm sorry, Mr. Barnaby," he said. "But, we need to look at the exterior of your station to make sure there aren't any more of those eggs attached."

As Mr. Barnaby operated the exterior cameras, he spotted hundreds of them.

"We may be able to destroy those eggs," Mr. Barnaby said.

"How?" the colonel asked.

"The onboard spacesuits are equipped with built-in lasers the crew used to remove debris from the station," Mr. Barnaby explained.

After the colonel exited the space station on a long leash, he fired the laser on a green egg. As it floated away, he found something concerning—the metal was soft.

"I'm coming back inside," he said.

He met with Mr. Barnaby.

"What's the problem, Colonel?" Mr. Barnaby asked.

"Those eggs exude a chemical that's is softening the metal on your hull, and in time, those creatures will be able to get inside, leaving us only one alternative," he said.

"Are you saying what I think you're saying?" Mr. Barnaby asked.

"I'm sorry, but there aren't any other options!" he stated. "If those creatures ever made it to Earth, there's no telling what would happen."

"If you're going to destroy my life's work, you can allow me to download the station data files," Mr. Barnaby said.

"How much time will that take?" he asked.

"About an hour," Mr. Barnaby replied.

"You do that while we set the explosives," he said.

Afterward, the team tried to reenter the control room, but they were locked out.

"Open the door, Mr. Barnaby," he asked.

"I'm sorry, colonel, but this was a one-way trip for me," Mr. Barnaby said.

"You'll die, Mr. Barnaby!" he yelled.

"I'm already a dead man, colonel," Mr. Barnaby exclaimed.

"Please reconsider, Mr. Barnaby," he asked.

"Only if you can stop the fatal disease ravaging my brain," Mr. Barnaby answered.

"Have it your way, Mr. Barnaby," he said.

On their way back to Earth, they witnessed a massive explosion. Four days later, they arrived back at NASA.

The colonel gave his condolences to Mr. Reeves.

A week later, part of the Barnaby Station reentered Earth's atmosphere and crashed within the Arizona Navajo reservation. Colonel Cooper and his team went to investigate. When they walked into the small town, they found mummified remains of tribal members, and he called NASA.

"Some of those creatures survived the crash," he said.

"What about the people on the reservation?" Mr. Reeves asked.

"All dead," the colonel answered.

Mr. Reeves called the Governor of Arizona, who dispatched a National Guard Unit. They arrived on the reservation a few hours later.

"Any idea why they sent us here, Lieutenant?" Sergeant Wilks asked.

"They told me to watch for unusual wildlife," he replied.

As he led his men up a hill, they heard strange screeching noises.

"What in the hell was that, Lieutenant?" Sergeant Wilks asked.

"No clue, so let's slowly back down this hill," he replied.

They soon saw what made the noise.

"What the fuck are those things, Lieutenant?" Sergeant Ames asked.

They shot several creatures, but in the end, they were all killed.

"What direction?" The colonel asked.
"Due east, colonel," Jacoby answered.
They found the National Guard unit.
"God damn it!" he exclaimed.
He called Mr. Reeves on the SAT phone. That's when he saw a group of creatures coming their way. As they ran back to town, he dropped the phone. When he and his team got there, they went inside the market with barred windows.
"What are we going to do now, colonel?" Jacoby asked.
"We can't stay in here," he replied. "So, I'll go outside to draw some of them in."
"Isn't that a bit risky," Jacoby warned.
"It is, but we need to thin the herd," he said.
He walked to the middle of the street and stood there. As five creatures slowly approached him, his team opened fire.
"While you were out, I found a working phone in the back," Jacoby said.
The colonel called Mr. Reeves about the National Guard Unit, and that they're pinned down by a group of creatures. He advised Mr. Reeves to have the military drop hellfire missiles to burn the entire town to the ground. Mr. Reeves called President Braithwaite, who reluctantly agreed, and he ordered two A-10's from Davis-Monthan Air Force Base.
"When we hear the A-10's coming in low, we run like hell!" he ordered.
About thirty minutes later, the planes were making their approach, and the team made a run for it. They ran through the herd of creatures, but Jacoby fell. The missiles incinerated most of the strange animals, but a few chased after the colonel and his men. As the team stopped to fight the creatures, the creatures stopped moving.
"Why did they stop?" Miller asked.
"I don't know," the colonel answered.

That's when they saw a much larger creature coming in the distance. After the smaller ones were dead, they turned their attention to the larger one, but their bullets did not affect it. As it closed in, an A-10 fired a missile. As the creature exploded, the colonel got covered in its acidic blood.

A few days later, he awoke in the hospital with Mr. Reeves at his side.

"How are you feeling, Colonel Cooper?" Mr. Reeves asked.

"Lucky to be alive, I guess," he said.

"After your accident, President Brathwaite authorized us to use alien bionics on you," Mr. Reeves said.

"Alien Bionics?" he asked.

"It was something our government recovered after the Roswell incident," Mr. Reeves said. "Since the surgeons couldn't save your left arm or legs, we had them replaced."

"Then why can I feel them?" he asked.

"We're not exactly sure how the artificial limbs work, but they reestablish lost neural pathways to your spinal cord," Mr. Reeves said.

"How much did that cost the government?" the colonel asked.

"Let's just say that you owe us a favor," Mr. Reeves answered.

The End

Writer's Block

JAKE MOSS, A horror novelist, developed writer's block, and for days, he just sat at his computer unable to type a word. So, he decided to take a vacation in his mountain cabin. While there, he went fishing and hiking to refresh his muddled mind.

One night, a strange whirring noise woke him from a deep sleep, and he got out of bed to see what was causing it. When he opened the door, he got blinded by a bright light.

The next morning, he thought he had dreamt the incident. As he hiked along a five-mile trail, he listened to his favorite music via headphones. Three hours later, he walked into his cabin and powered up his laptop.

As he was typing, he still had on his headphones, and he didn't hear the fire-breathing dragon approach his cabin. The exact time he decided to write about another kind of monster as he held down the delete key. He called his new creation a 'Blood Beast.' As he began the macabre tale of the invisible blood beast, it was slowly approaching its first victim. That's when he felt a presence behind him. As he turned to look, he was holding down the delete key. He then smelt a pungent odor and opened the door to air out his cabin. That's when he noticed the smell of smoke, but he didn't see any.

After the odor had dissipated, he decided to have lunch. While he sat in front of his laptop, ideas for a different genre popped into his head. He had always dreamed about writing a spy novel about the woman who sometimes haunted his dreams. He then began writing about the mysterious Sheila North, a tall, seductive assassin with emerald green eyes and jet-black hair.

An hour later, he was startled by a knock on his door. As he opened the door, a beautiful woman was standing there, and she told him that someone was following her.

"You'll be safe here," he said.

That evening, they talked about their dreams, loves, and passions, and then they made love.

In the morning, he smiled as he looked at the woman in his bed. He had never met such a beautiful woman and decided to delete his Sheila North story. As he held down the delete key, she vanished right before his eyes, and the aliens laughed at their prank.

The End

Martian Mud Pie

On January 10, 2037, the Joint Space Exploration Program comprised of China, Russia, and the United States launched its first mission to Mars with the crew of Commander Jake Blade; Co-pilot Leo Popov; Science Officer, Bai Liu; Flight Engineer, Jason Miller; Astrobiologist Mylon Bianchi; and Archeologist, Henry Smith.

On September 28, 2037, they landed on Mars near the Cydonia Region. Their mission–to search for signs of ancient alien life.

The next day, two rovers exited the ship — the first with Henry and Jason, and the other with Bai and Mylon to study a canyon.

Henry and Jason used hand-held radar devices searching for alien artifacts while Bai and Mylon investigated the canyon. Bai and Mylon found nothing more than strange-looking rock formations that resembled trees. After they exited the rover, they spotted a cave. When they went inside, they didn't feel the slight tingle caused by a protective force field. The cave had luminescent crystals lighting the walls, but what they saw next astounded them. There were words etched into the wall.

"We need Henry to look at this writing," Mylon said.

"Team Alpha, do you copy?" Bai asked.

"Team Alpha," Henry replied.

"We found writing of some kind on a cave wall, and we need you to look at it," Bai said.

"We'll be there tomorrow," Henry said excitedly. "Team Alpha, out."

"My readings say that the air in here is breathable," Mylon answered.

"That's impossible!" Bai said.

Mylon removed her helmet, took a deep breath. Bai did the same.

"How can we be breathing Earth-like air?" Bai asked.

"I believe…Mylon began, but she was interrupted.

"Do you hear that?" Bai asked.

"Hear what?" Mylon asked.

"Listen," Bai said.

"I hear a low-pitched whine?" Mylon said.

"Where's it coming from?" Bai asked.

As they walked deeper into the cave, the sound grew louder, and Mylon spotted something moving. They approached the object, which looked like a mud pie with four strange-looking plants sticking out of it, weaving back and forth.

"What is it?" Bai asked.

"It appears to be some form of plant life," Mylon answered.

Bai touched it.

"It shocked me!" she yelled.

Mylon also touched it out of curiosity and received a similar shock.

It was time for their sleep cycle, and they returned to their rover. As Bai and Mylon slept, they dreamt of being in ancient Greece with people bowing down to them.

They awoke the next day, noting that they had slept fifteen hours.

"Why did we sleep for so long?" Bai asked.

"I don't know, but I feel fantastic," Mylon said.

"I do, too," Bai said.

They walked back into the cave, removed their helmets, and spacesuits.

An hour later, Henry and Jason were surprised to see them out of their spacesuits.

"It's safe," Mylon said.

Henry and Jason removed theirs as well.

"Where's the writing you wanted me to see?" Henry asked.

They pointed to the wall.

When Henry looked at them, he was shocked.

"Impossible?" Henry exclaimed. "It's ancient Greek."

"Can you read it?" Jason asked.

"To all who enter, beware. Four gods, who have wronged humanity, have been imprisoned in a field of sorrow," Henry read.

When they turned around, Bai and Mylon's eyes were glowing.

"Bai, Mylon, what happened to you?" Jason asked.

"They're no longer with us," the voices said.

When they touched Henry and Jason, they released two other Gods from their prison, and then they made love with their new bodies. Three hours later, they approached their ship without their spacesuits.

"Commander, the crew is returning without their spacesuits," Leo said.

"Prepare for emergency takeoff," Jake yelled.

After the ship was forced back down onto Mars, the four gods boarded, and they tossed Jake and Leo outside, where they died instantly. The spacecraft sped towards earth at an unbelievable rate of speed, and a few days later, it crashed into the Mediterranean Sea. When NASA recovered the ship, no one was inside. The rescue crew could see lightning on Mount Olympus as Apollo, Aphrodite, Athena, and Hermes rebuilt their kingdom while Bai, Henry, Jason, and Mylon suffered a fate worse than death—stuck in a Martian Mud Pie.

The End

Death's Apprentice

I DIED WHEN TWO men tried to shoot a woman sitting at the next table, and foolishly I shielded her. As I laid on the ground, dying, she shot the men and walked away.

When I awoke, I found myself on a bed in an unfamiliar room. As I sat up, a woman walked in and told me to put on the suit hanging in the closet.

"Why?" I asked.

"For your meeting with the 'Man in Charge,'" she replied.

"Who?" I asked.

She didn't respond as she left the room. I did as she asked, and oddly, the suit fit me perfectly. As I walked outside the room, she told me to take the elevator to the tenth floor. I pushed the button, and as soon as the door closed, it reopened again. As I exited, a man pointed to a room, and when I entered, a man named Peter was sitting behind a desk.

"Why am I here?" I asked.

"For your afterlife assignment, Mr. Thomas," he explained.

"So, my death wasn't a dream?" I asked.

"I'm afraid not Mr. Thomas because the woman you protected should be the one sitting across from me!" he stated.

"Why?" I asked curiously.

"Because she's an assassin, and she would have been perfect for this assignment," he said.

"Is she supposed to kill someone?" I asked.

"In a manner of speaking," he replied.

"If this is the afterlife, why would there be a need for an assassin?" I asked.

He avoided the question.

"The man upstairs has authorized me to make you a one-time offer since you shouldn't be here," he said.

"What kind of offer?" I asked.

"If you touch the female assassin with this crystal, you can take her place," he said.

"What?" I growled. "I was a man on Earth!"

"I'm sorry, but we don't have spare bodies just lying around," he said.

"You don't make it easy, do you?" I asked.

"I assure you that you will be well-compensated for your troubles," he replied.

It took me a year to find the assassin inside a hotel bathroom.

"Remember me, bitch?" I asked rudely.

"How did you get in here? Wait...you died at that restaurant," she said.

"I did die, saving your worthless ass," I replied.

I touched her with the crystal, and suddenly I was inside her body. That's when Peter appeared.

"Why are you here?" I asked.

"The man upstairs told me to add an addendum onto your contract," he said.

"What kind of addendum?" I asked.

"You will be our Earth-bound assassin for terminating evil people," he said.

"Anything else I should know?" I asked.

"You're now immortal, and Natalia Kuznetsov was a lesbian," Peter said.

I smiled.

"Just out of curiosity, if I had stayed with you, what would have been my assignment?" I asked.

"You would have been Death's apprentice," he answered.

I laughed at the irony as he handed me a packet.

"This is your first assignment," he said.

"Can't I get adjusted to my new body first?" I asked.

"You have six months to complete it," he replied.

After I opened the packet, I couldn't help but laugh because the two people had a lot to answer for in their political careers.

"How do I pay for my expenses?" I asked.

"Here's your bank book, and the PIN Number to access your money," he replied.

"That's a lot of money," I said.

"The Man said that you're entitled to it, so enjoy your new life," he said.

He vanished, and I thought I was alone until the most beautiful woman walked in.

"Who were you talking to Natalia?" she asked me.

"Just concluding some old business," I answered. "Now, where were we?"

The End

Mind Games

As SIXTY-FIVE-YEAR-OLD AUTHOR Alexander Fleming typed his latest detective novel, someone opened his patio door. After hearing someone say, "find him," he hid.

As four men searched his home, they finally found him inside his office closet.

"Do you have a name, buddy?" Hawke asked.

"Alexander Fleming, but what do you want with me?" he asked nervously.

"We're not looking for you, Mr. Fleming. We're looking for an assassin," Hawke said.

"Why would an assassin be living here with me?" he asked.

"I am sorry, but we received bad Intel," Hawke said.

"What's going to happen to me?" he asked.

"I'm sorry, but we can't leave witnesses behind!" he stated.

"Since I am going to die, does your assassin have a name?" he asked.

"Sebastian Blade," Hawke said.

Hawke unintentionally awoke something deadly inside Alexander Fleming. After he killed the four men, the bruised and battered Sebastian Blade made a call.

"Code Name 'Blade,'" he said.

"How the hell did you get activated, Sebastian?" Mr. Athos asked.

"Four men tried to kill me, and they nearly succeeded because you put me in some old fuck's body," he asked.

"The person with your consciousness was critically injured in a car accident, and I was forced to act quickly. I found the old man in the same emergency room and put you inside of him," Mr. Athos explained. "But soon, you'll be reunited with your body when it's out of cryogenic stasis."

"Until then, what do I do?" he asked.

"I dispatched a team to your location," Mr. Athos replied.

An hour later, as two men poured accelerant throughout the house, a woman placed a mind retrieval device on Alexander Fleming to retrieve Sebastian Blade's consciousness. Mr. Fleming suddenly found himself sitting in his chair.

"Who are you, and where are those men?" he asked.

"They were gone when we arrived, so if you want to survive, you'll need a new identity," she lied.

"Like WITSEC?" he asked.

"What we do, Mr. Fleming is far more advanced," she stated. "Along with your new identity comes a new body."

She placed the device on his head, and after a few moments, his body slumped in the chair. When the fire department arrived at the house, the only thing they could do was to keep the fire from spreading.

Two days later, Mr. Fleming emerged as forty-year-old William Anders. But, he had no clue that the same woman had retrieved Mr. Anders's consciousness before his because he was dying from brain cancer. To live a longer life, Mr. Anders paid Mr. Athos ten million dollars, and the rest went to Callum Reed, his new identity. They kidnapped Mr. Reed at his request and replaced his mind with his.

Three months later, Mr. Anders was in the hospital dying, but before he died, an organization called the Sentinels retrieved his consciousness. When he awoke, he was sitting across from two people.

"Mr. Anders, have you been approached by Mr. Athos?" a woman asked.

"I'm sorry, but I'm not Mr. Anders," he answered.

"Then who the hell are you?" a man asked angrily.

"Alexander Fleming, the writer," he replied.

"How did you end up in Mr. Anders?" she asked.

"Mr. Athos put me in his body after his people saved me from four assassins," he said.

"Why were they after you?" the man asked.

"They weren't after me, but someone named Sebastian Blade," he answered.

The man told the woman to meet him outside.

"We now know what happened to Hawke's team, and he doesn't have a clue," the man said.

"Maybe, he knows more than you think," she suggested.

They walked back into the room to resume their questioning.

"After they saved you, where did they take you?" she asked.

"To some strange laboratory," he said.

"What do you mean by strange?" she asked.

"There were two frozen bodies inside two chambers," he said. "I overheard Mr. Athos talking about Callum Reed, who I believe was one of those bodies."

The man beckoned the woman outside the room again.

"It's apparent that Mr. Anders now occupies Callum Reed's body. The other body must have been Sebastian Blade," he said.

"We'll take care of them later, but first, we must find and destroy Mr. Athos' mind retrieval devices before he can create an army of hidden assassins," she said.

"What are we going to do with Mr. Fleming?" the man asked.

"I think his near-death experience could work in our favor," she said.

"We let him walk if he kills Mr. Athos?" the man asked.

"You got it," she said.

They walked back into the room.

"We have a proposition for you, Mr. Fleming," she said.

"Let me guess. If I want to live, I must kill someone for you?" Mr. Fleming asked.

"That someone would be Mr. Athos," she said.

"Instead of killing him, I have a more creative idea in mind for that bastard," he said. "You should place his mind inside one of the female apes at the zoo."

The two agents laughed at the absurdity of his idea, but they liked it.

He took them to the lab, where Mr. Athos transferred his mind to Mr. Ander's body. When they got there, the lab was gone, but they found a change of address letter from the Post office.

Two days later, they drove past the new address and parked up the street to watch. As they watched the house through binoculars, the man saw Mr. Athos and Sebastian Blade walk outside arguing about something.

"It's time, Mr. Fleming," she said.

He walked up to the house dressed as a mailman and shot them with tranquilizer darts.

The next morning, Mr. Athos and Sebastian Blade woke inside a cage with people laughing and staring at them.

The Sentinels destroyed Mr. Athos' devices; Mr. Reed committed suicide, and Mr. Fleming became William Forsythe, a young detective novel writer.

The End

The Murder Witness

As SARAH ADLER watched, her family was murdered one by one while under the protection of the U.S. Marshals Service. Her father, William, worked for Charles Gaspar as an accountant when he discovered financial irregularities. He knew what they meant and reported them to the FBI. He and his family were moved to a safe house as the FBI built a case against Charles Gaspar.

As Sarah lay dying, a mythical being bit her and then dripped blood into her mouth. The next morning, the marshals protecting the Adler family hadn't reported in as required. When the police arrived, they found two marshals—one dead and the other wounded. They also found Sarah Adler alive, but barely.

Special Agents, Rob Prentiss, and Jason Poole arrived on the crime scene.

"How did this happen?" Agent Prentiss asked.

"There must be a leak inside the U.S. Marshal's Service," Agent Poole suggested.

Agent Prentiss called the U.S. Marshal's Service.

"I was briefed this morning about the situation," Director Stevens said.

"I believe there's a leak inside your organization," he stated.

"And we both know who, so do what you need to do!" the director said.

Agent Prentiss contacted an FBI forensic accountant, and she found an offshore bank in the name of Walter Williams—the wounded U.S. Marshal. He went to the hospital to confront him.

"I'm here to discuss your offshore bank account, Marshal Williams!" Agent Prentiss said.

Marshal Williams' face suddenly went pale.

"Director Stevens and I know you were the leak," Agent Prentiss said.

"I'm sorry, but Charles Gaspar threatened to kill my family," he said.

"You could have talked to Director Stevens," Agent Prentiss said.

A nurse walked into the room and told Agent Prentiss that Sarah Adler died. Agent Prentiss read Marshal Williams his rights and handcuffed him to the bed. He then walked out to call the Chief of Police to post a guard outside his door, and then he called Director Stevens.

After a long day, Rob was downing vodka shots when he received word that someone killed Marshal Williams.

When he walked into the hospital room, he saw that Marshal Williams' head was missing from his body. As he looked out the window, no one could have gotten inside unless they propelled down by rope.

"Where's the officer posted outside the door?" Agent Prentiss asked a nurse.

"He's in a psychiatry holding cell," the nurse told him.

"Why?" he asked.

"He said that Sarah Adler killed Marshal Williams, and then he had to be sedated," she said.

"I need to talk to him," he said.

"You need the approval of his Psychiatrist, Dr. Lambert," she said.

"Where do I find Dr. Lambert?" he asked.

"She's over there writing doctor's orders," she said.

He went to talk to Dr. Lambert. When she turned around, she was strikingly beautiful.

"Can I help you?" Dr. Lambert asked.

"I...er..," he said.

"For some reason, I get that a lot," she admitted.

"I'm Agent Prentiss from the FBI, and I need to speak with the police officer who witnessed Marshal William's murder," he said.

"If you want to interview him, I must accompany you," she said.

Two hours earlier, Marshal Williams was contemplating prison when Sarah Adler appeared inside his room.

"Hello, Marshal Williams!" Sarah said.

"You can't be real because you died today," he said.

"I did die, thanks to you. But why my family?" she asked.

"Charles Gaspar threatened to kill my family if I didn't do as he asked," he said.

"So, to protect your family, mine had to die?" she asked quizzically.

"I'm truly sorry," he said.

"It's too late for sorry, Marshal Williams," she said.

The police officer posted outside his room, heard his screams, and when he entered the room, Sarah Adler finished ripping Marshal Williams' head off his body, and then she exited out the window.

Agent Prentiss and Doctor Lambert arrived at the holding cells to question the officer.

"I'm here to ask you about Marshal Williams' murder," Agent Prentiss said.

"I swear, it was Sarah Adler, and then she walked out the window," the officer responded.

"This girl?" he showed him her picture.

"Yes, that's her," the officer said.

"What you're telling me is impossible because she died earlier today," he stated.

"She's dead?" he asked sadly.

As the officer cried, he stopped the questioning.

The next day, Agent Prentiss got a call from Agent Poole about the Marshal Williams' family, and they met at the crime scene.

"Do you think Gaspar is behind these murders?" he asked.

"Yes, but the trail will never lead back to him," Agent Poole said.

"I think we should interview him," Agent Prentiss said.

"He's all lawyered up, so we can't," Agent Poole said.

Two days later, Agent Prentiss received a call about a man missing his head in a warehouse.

"I'll be there in one hour," Agent Prentiss said.

He tried to call Agent Poole, but it went straight to voicemail, so he went to the warehouse alone. After he went inside, he found the dead man, realizing it was Agent Poole and knelt beside his body. Just then, Charles Gaspar told Agent Prentiss to stand up and turn around.

"Why did you kill my friend?" he asked.

"Just tying up a few loose ends," Charles Gaspar said.

As Charles Gaspar was about to shoot Agent Prentiss, he heard gunshots, and then a man screamed.

"What the fuck was that," Charles Gaspar said.

As he looked away momentarily, Agent Prentiss quickly went on the offensive, and they wrestled for the gun, and it went off, hitting Agent Prentiss in the shoulder, but he still took Charles Gaspar down. Afterward, Agent Prentiss made Charles Gaspar walk in front of him.

As they headed to the exit, they heard more gunfire and another man screaming.

"What the fuck is happening?" Gaspar yelled.

"You tell me!" Agent Prentiss said.

As they continued towards the exit, they found another man missing his head.

"Who's killing my men?" Gaspar yelled.

Suddenly, Sarah Adler appeared.

"Charles Gaspar fooled you into coming here, so he could kill you like Agent Poole," Sarah said. "I'm sorry that I wasn't able to save your friend."

"The nurse told me that you died," he said.

"I hate to burst your pragmatic bubble Agent Prentiss, but I am no longer human," Sarah said.

She then attacked Charles Gaspar, but in doing so, she knocked Agent Prentiss unconscious, and then she ripped off Charles Gaspar's head. When Agent Prentiss woke, he was inside an ambulance with a letter sitting on top of him, and he opened it.

Agent Prentiss, I must apologize for pretending to be Dr. Lambert, and for Sarah because she didn't mean to hurt you. You see, she is now like me because I saved her on the night Charles Gaspar's men murdered her family. You're probably unaware that my kind does not harm the innocent. After I met you, Sarah and I agreed to watch over you. When she killed Charles Gaspar, and some of his men, the others scattered to the wind, but we will find them and punish them. I know you have questions, but there are things in this world you could never accept nor understand, and so, it would be best to forget that we ever met. As she told you, Sarah is no longer human, so please allow her to remain dead and buried.

The End

The Detective's Alter Ego

G*AMEPLAY,* **THE LARGEST** video game developer in the United States, wanted to take their gaming to the next level. In their search, they found and hired Silas Vonner, an unknown programmer, who had something different to offer them.

Until recently, he was a Professor of Quantum Physics at MIT but resigned because his theories conflicted with the status quo.

After leaving MIT, he chose video game programming as his new vocation.

On his first day at *Gameplay*, they took him to his lab replete with scientific equipment. After looking everything over, he requested some additional items for a device he wanted to build. Once he had everything in place, he constructed an Atomic Compositor with 7D holographic imaging technology that allows atoms inside an electromagnetic field to make game characters appear real for fixing programming flaws.

He then began designing the new *Gameplay* console to provide a realistic interactive gaming environment without the need for virtual glasses. Once he completed it, he requested a female employee to help him with simulations.

A week later, he sent the female employee home early, and then he took the console to the room adjacent to his lab, where he switched the signs.

He called his supervisors and then turned on the console. When they walked into the lab, they didn't realize that they were inside a video game.

"Why did you need to see us, Silas?" Mr. Archer asked.

"Because Ms. Reynolds is quite upset," he said.

"What's wrong, Ms. Reynolds?" Mr. Miller asked.

"I've been with *Gameplay* for five years, and I haven't received one raise," she said.

"This isn't the proper venue to discuss a raise," Mr. Miller said.

"I think it's now or never," she said with a gun pointed at Silas.

"There's no need for violence, Ms. Reynolds!" Mr. Benton yelled.

She shot Silas, who just stood there smiling.

"Why would you allow her to do that?" Mr. Miller yelled.

"You mean, Ms. Reynolds?" he asked. "I sent her home two hours ago, so thank you for participating in my game simulation."

"You mean, she isn't real?" Mr. Archer asked.

"Neither is the lab you're standing in," he said. "Welcome to AI gaming."

"This would put us light years ahead of our competition," Mr. Archer said.

"I knew you'd like it, but it's time to do what you hired me to do. I want to design a game called *The Detective's Alter Ego*," he said.

"What would it entail?" Mr. Miller asked.

"It's about a private investigator, who has an assassin alter ego," he said. "I believe gamers would find it fun because it would allow them to become or interact with either character."

"I'm giving you the green light," Mr. Archer said.

To begin developing *The Detective's Alter Ego*, Silas wrote profiles for Tammie Marshall, Private Investigator, and the assassin, Sonya Danvers.

Tammie Marshall

Physical Description: Shoulder length auburn hair; blue eyes; forty years of age; 5' feet 6" inches tall; medium build; toned physique; little make-up; and wears pantsuits.

Personality Description: An independent woman who considers herself one of the good guys; and, she is unstoppable when investigating a case.

Background: Canadian, but resides in Texas where she operates Marshall Investigations; she carries a 9 mm Glock in a shoulder holster, and rides a Harley Davidson Motorcycle she calls Slim.

Sonya Danvers

Physical Description: Shoulder length red hair; emerald green eyes; wears gold shimmering eye shadow; 5' feet 6" inches tall; medium build; muscular physique; thirty-five years of age; and, she wears a black and gold leather one-piece motorcycle suit with a matching helmet.

Personality Description: Drinks Jose Cuervo Especial; when she's on the make, she wears a black mini-skirt and matching top. Sometimes she uses her body to lure victims to their death after she gets what she wants.

Background: From Dublin, Ireland, where a bomb killed her family; at eighteen, she was a professional motorcycle racer; at twenty-two, she was taken by *The Hands of Death* to an island for assassin training. Instead of resisting, she relished the training to become a world-class assassin; she wears a double shoulder holster with two Akai handguns; and, she rides a black and gold Kawasaki Ninja H2R.

After completing the profiles, he began writing a program to bring them to life. It took him a year and was now ready to load his program into the atomic compositor. After he turned it on, Tammie Marshall appeared, and then he switched to Sonya Danvers. After Silas examined each character, they were perfect. Now, he had to design a world for them to live.

That night, he was so exhausted that he fell asleep on his couch at home. As he slept, a fierce thunderstorm caused a massive power surge at *Gameplay*, damaging the atomic compositor. A security guard heard an explosion and went to investigate. When he walked into the lab where Silas worked, a woman was standing beside the atomic compositor.

"You shouldn't be in here, Ma'am?" he asked.

"I think you'll do for now!" she said.

"She grabbed him by the tie, dragged him to a chair, pulled down his pants, and then straddled him.

"Strangely pleasurable," she said.

After it was over, she knocked him unconscious.

Afterward, she left the building, reached her arms out, and a black and gold Kawasaki Ninja H2R with a matching helmet appeared. The mini-skirt and matching top became a one-piece black and gold leather suit, and then she rode away.

The next morning when Silas went to his lab, he found the security guard rubbing his jaw.

"What the hell happened?" Silas asked.

"There was an explosion, and I came to investigate. When I walked in, I found a woman standing there," he pointed.

"A woman?" Silas asked. "What did she look like?"

"She had red hair, green eyes, and she was wearing a black mini-skirt," he said.

"What did she do?" Silas asked.

"She used me, and then she hit me," he said.

He told him to report to the clinic.

When Silas checked his program, it was gone.

"What have I done?" he said.

That afternoon, Sonya went to a bar and ordered several shots of Jose Cuervo Especial. That evening she went to a motel with a middle-aged man who paid her bar tab.

As she awoke the next morning, he was looking her over, which angered her, and she broke his neck. She put his body in the shower and positioned it to make it appear as a freak accident. She looked inside his wallet to find $800 in cash, credit cards, a debit card, and a realtor business card. She took the money and one of his cards. She then left the motel on her motorcycle. When she saw a bank, she pulled into the parking lot. She opened a joint checking account in her name and Tammie Marshall, but she didn't understand why. She deposited $800.00 and then asked for two debit cards.

Afterward, she found a computer repair shop because she needed a laptop to advertise her services on the dark web. When she walked inside, she told the employee precisely what she wanted. He brought out three laptops. She didn't like the first two, but she did like the third. He told her that the computer would cost her $1,000 because of the software on it. She told him to lock the door, and she would please him for a discount. When they went into the back, she killed him with a Dim Mak death blow. She made his death look like an accident, and then she fled with the laptop. She then went to a nearby motel with Wi-Fi.

She wrote a computer program to siphon money into her checking account from illegal offshore bank accounts. She knew no one would object because she wasn't taking large sums of money from their ill-gotten gains. A few minutes later, she had $200,000 in her checking. She then went onto the Dark Web to advertise her services. As she napped, she changed back into Tammie Marshall, who was startled by her location but was aware of her strange blackouts. She knew the clothing inside the closet belonged to her alter ego. That's how Silas programmed her. She opened her new laptop to find local building rentals for opening Marshall Investigations, but first, she had to check her bank account, where she found $200,000, which didn't surprise her any. She spotted the real estate business card on the nightstand, and she called the number.

"Walter Properties, how may I assist you?" a receptionist asked.

"My name is Tammie Marshall, may I speak to Richard Conner," she asked.

"I'm sorry, Ms. Marshall, he isn't available," the receptionist said. "Would you like to speak to Sharon Porter?"

"Sure, that would be great," she said.

"This is Sharon; how may I help you, Ms. Marshall?" she asked.

"I'm looking for a rental property to open my private investigation services," she said.

"How big?" Sharon asked.

"Small because I work alone," she said.

"I do have three properties for you to view, would tomorrow work for you?" Sharon asked.

"What time?" she asked.

"Would 10:00 am work for you?" Sharon asked.

"Yes, I'll see you then," she said.

After Tammie fell asleep, Sonya awoke to check for job offers on the Dark Web. She had one for a Silas Vonner, an employee at *Gameplay*, which pays $100,000. Sonya wondered who wanted him dead, so she tracked the offer to Mr. Benton, who also works at *Gameplay*, which made her further curious. She looked into his financials, to find a large payment in his offshore bank account from *Game Works* and to find that he works for the same company.

Silas received a text from Sonya saying that Mr. Benton wanted him dead. She told him to stay hidden until further notice and then rode her motorcycle to Mr. Benton's mansion. After climbing over his wall, two large dogs attacked her, and Sonya knocked them unconscious. She found an open window and crawled inside, where she heard someone talking on the phone.

"Soon, we won't have to worry about Silas Vonner any longer," Mr. Benton said.

The other person asked a question.

"I don't know, but she comes highly recommended," he said. "When Silas is dead, I'll call you."

After hanging up, he was startled by Sonya's voice.

"You mean assassinated, Mr. Benton?" she asked.

"Who the fuck are you?" he asked.

"Sonya Danvers, the assassin you hired," she said.

"Why does that name sound familiar?" he asked.

"I never mentioned my name on the Dark Web," she said.

"How the hell did you find me?" he asked.

"We all have our little secrets, don't we, Mr. Benton. Yours is that you're employed by *Game Works*, working as a spy at *Gameplay*," she said.

"Now, I remember Sonya Danvers. She's the assassin in that alter ego game designed by Mr. Vonner at *Gameplay*," he said

"How strange! I left there last night, but I have no clue why I was there," she said.

"There is no way you could exist!" he said.

"I am here, aren't I? Now, where's the money?"

"In the bag over there," he said.

"There is one more thing you should know, Mr. Benton!" she stated.

"And what is that?" he asked.

"That I have one ethical rule about assassinations," she said. "I never sanction people in a competitive environment unless the competitor plays dirty like *Game Works*."

"What does that mean!" he said.

"It means that I will be ending your life instead of Mr. Vonner," she said.

His eyes grew wide, and then she shot him.

She took the money and left the way she came in. She then returned to the motel to find the other person on the other end of his call. She opened the laptop to view Mr. Benton's phone records. It took her only a few moments to locate Fred Stanton, the CEO of *Game Works*. She rode her motorcycle close to his mansion and parked. Getting into the estate was easy until she got into a firefight with his security team. Afterward, she found him hiding inside a panic room, and she left upon hearing sirens. As she ran to her motorcycle, the police cruisers were coming in both directions, and in the blink of an eye, she changed back into Tammie Marshall. The police took her to Mr. Stanton.

"That's not her," Mr. Stanton said.

"Are you positive?" the police officer asked.

"The woman had red hair, green eyes, and two guns, so yes, I'm positive," he said.

"Ma'am, why were you parked on the vacant property driveway?" the officer asked.

"I wasn't parked, my motorcycle stalled," she said.

Tammie knew it had something to do with her alter ego, but why was she after Mr. Stanton.

The next morning, Ms. Porter showed her three properties, and she found one that she liked. She paid her rent six months in advance, and then she called a company to print her business cards and one for her building signage.

After returning to the motel, she found the file belonging to Sonya Danvers, and she opened it. She now understood why Sonya was after Mr. Stanton, and she called Silas Vonner.

"Who is this?" he asked.

"Tammie Marshall, a private investigator," she said.

"How did you get my number?" he asked.

"It makes no difference, but your life is in danger!" she stated.

"I know," he said. "Sonya Danvers told me."

"What did she tell you to do?" she asked.

"To hide until she calls," he said.

"Do what she says," she said. "In the meantime, I'll look into Mr. Stanton."

The CEO of *Game Works*?" he asked.

"He's the one, who paid Mr. Benton to hire an assassin," she said.

She started digging into Mr. Stanton's financials and business dealings. She sent what she found to the FBI, and they arrested him.

As she laid down to rest, she knew her alter ego would take care of Mr. Stanton. Two hours later, Sonya woke with a vengeance to find where they were holding Mr. Stanton and disguised herself as Agent Moore, a blonde with blue eyes. When she walked by his cell, she shot him with a poisoned dart, and he began gasping and turning blue. After several agents rushed into the cell, she pretended to feel for his pulse, but she was removing the poisoned dart.

"He's dead!" Agent Moore stated.

Agent Moore vanished as quickly as she appeared.

Afterward, she called Silas.

"Thank you for saving my life, Sonya," he said.

"No problem, but this is the last time that we will speak," she said.

"Understood," he said.

He decided to dismantle the Atomic Compositor and do the programming the old-fashioned way because he didn't want any more of his creations running amok.

A year later, his game *The Detective's Alter Ego* with his console was a massive hit amongst gamers, which allows them to become or interact with the characters in a realistic environment.

Tammie Marshall was now running a successful investigative service, and Sonya continued to do what she did.

The End

Last Stand Alaska

"THE BEGINNING OF the end began in 2019 when Earth's weather patterns suddenly shifted without warning. The abrupt shift caused increased earthquake activity and several volcanoes to erupt. Two years later, two massive earthquakes, followed by several significant quakes, killed thousands upon thousands of people in several countries. The first two earthquakes were so powerful that two tectonic plates cracked under pressure causing the Earth to shift off its axis further. But, the United States did not go unscathed as two volcanoes on Hawaii, Kilauea and Mauna Loa, exploded without warning killing thousands of people. However, our disasters didn't end. Almost a year later, a hundred-foot wall of water hit the Atlantic Seaboard, killing more than twenty million Americans, and the scientific community had no explanation.

"In 2024, rumors circulated about Black Widow Spiders being the size of tarantulas, which was readily dismissed by the science community. Several months later, they were the size of large dogs, making them a threat to our survival.

"On February 25, 2025, I was forced to flee my home when a group of spiders broke through my front window. After getting into my SUV, I drove to the nearby Walmart because it had a walk-in milk cooler, where I can stay safe until the outdoor temperature drops. When the spiders stop moving, I'll head north to Flagstaff, Arizona.

"As I parked close to the automatic doors at Walmart, several spiders were approaching. After I pried the doors open with a crowbar, a few got inside before the doors reclosed. As fate would have it, I saved five people by pulling them into the walk-in cooler with me."

After Jessica stopped writing, a woman named Alice asked her about it.

"I've been writing in this journal since 2019, hoping that someone in the future will understand why the world went crazy after my death," Jessica said.

"You think we're going to die?" Matthew asked.

"I was referring to my death in old age," she said. "So, relax, we'll be leaving here soon."

"Who made you the leader?" Steven asked.

"As I see it, you five have three choices: You can stay in here and die from hypothermia; you can go out unarmed, and die a horrible death; or, you can stay with me to survive," she stated.

"She's right," Alice said.

Everyone agreed.

"I believe we should introduce ourselves," she said.

"Alice," she waved.

"Steven," he said.

"John," he said.

"Joyce," she said.

"Matthew," he said.

"And I'm Jessica," she said. "Before we leave here tonight, we'll need a few items, but we're stuck in here until the outside temperature drops below 60 degrees."

"Why?" Matthew asked.

"When the temperature drops to 60 degrees, the spiders don't move," she said.

"Are you a spider expert?" Matthew asked.

"No, but I've been studying their behavior," she said.

"You're gambling with our lives over a theory?" Matthew yelled.

She walked to the door and opened it. Outside, there were three spiders. "Come look if you don't believe me!" she said.

Everyone took a turn.

"Sorry, I doubted you," Matthew said.

"It understandable," she said.

"Once we leave here, where are we going?" Alice asked.

"North to Flagstaff," she said.

"Why there?" John asked.

"Because it's colder, which gives me time to plan for my Alaska trip," she said.

"Alaska!" Alice asked.

"I'm going there because it's part of the Arctic Circle where it's cold year 'round," she said.

"Oh no! My girlfriend!" Alice said, sadly.

"Where does she live?" Jessica asked.

"Tempe," Alice said.

"I think the phone lines are still active, so we need to find a phone, and if she answers, tell her to meet us in Flagstaff, but if she doesn't, the decision to stay behind is yours," she said.

Suddenly, John collapsed on the floor.

"He doesn't have a pulse, and he's not breathing!" Matthew said.

"I'll do the breathing while you do the chest compressions," Jessica stated.

They worked on him for a half-hour, trading positions, but he was gone.

"I'm sorry, but we tried," she said.

"How sad!" Alice said.

"He must have had a bad heart," she said.

"What are we going to do with his body?" Joyce asked.

"There isn't anything we can do, but leave him behind," she said.

"How much longer do we have to remain in here?" Matthew asked.

"About fifteen more minutes," she said.

"Good, because I'm freezing my ass off," Matthew said.

"Aren't we all," Joyce said.

Alice asked Jessica a question to keep everyone's minds occupied.

"Jessica, have you ever been to Alaska?" Alice asked.

"I was stationed at Fort Wainwright next to Fairbanks when I was in the Army," she said. But getting there may prove dangerous."

"Why?" Joyce asked.

"When the weather patterns shifted in 2019, and again in 2021, Utah and Idaho, and parts of Alberta and British Columbia began getting warm. Since I'm not leaving Flagstaff until May, I'm not sure what I'll run into when I drive to Alaska," she confided.

"Isn't there another route?" Joyce asked.

"Without a plane, the Alcan Highway is the only way to get there," she said.

"What items do we need?" Steven asked.

"We need backpacks, shotguns with two boxes of shells, canteens, peanut butter, a box of saltine crackers in case we get stranded, long johns, and a jacket, but first, there's a spider problem I need to rectify," she said.

After she killed five spiders, she returned.

"We need to divide and conquer to get our items faster," she said. "There will be three teams, and each team will need a shopping cart. Joyce and Alice get the crackers and peanut butter; Matthew and Steven, the backpacks and canteens; and I'll get the guns and the shells. Once you have those items, meet me at the entertainment department."

Everyone completed their first task.

"Our next task is to get ourselves long underwear, a winter jacket, and put them all on for our trip up north," she said.

A half-hour later, everyone returned to the Entertainment Department.

"Okay, Alice, it's time to make that call," she said. "You three get the water to fill the canteens while we find a phone."

After the last canteen was full, they returned with Alice smiling.

"So, I guess your girlfriend was home?" Steven asked.

"She was, and she's on her way to Flagstaff," Alice said happily.

"Have any of you ever shot a gun before?" she asked.

They all answered no.

"Shotguns are the easiest guns to load and use," she said.

She taught them how to load, shoot, and carry them properly.

"Grab your packs, it's time to go," she said. "My SUV is parked outside the door. I'll go out first to make sure it's safe."

When she went out, the spiders weren't moving, and she waved. Everyone hurried outside, put their backpacks and canteens in the back of her SUV, and then got inside. As they traveled north on I17, the drive was slow because they had to avoid abandoned vehicles along the way. It took them nearly three hours for the usual one-hour trip to Camp Verde.

"Tonight, we'll stay at the Cliff Castle Casino Hotel in two connected rooms," she said.

Later, they found Johnny Rocket's, where they made hamburgers and fries. Afterward, they made their way to the cashier's cage, grabbed some cash, and sat on a row of slot machines. Steven hit the jackpot as he played Bonnie and Clyde.

"Just my luck! I finally win big, and there's no payout," Steven said.

Everyone laughed.

After an hour, they went to their rooms.

The next morning, the temperature was warmer than expected.

"We need to move quickly, its already 75 degrees outside," she stated.

Everyone scrambled to the SUV. As they hit the I17 toward Flagstaff, a group of spiders was moving across the freeway, but the sound of her engine attracted them.

"Shit!" Jessica exclaimed.

"Can't you go drive through them?" Matthew asked.

"There's too many, so we need to thin the herd. Steven, go right, Matthew, left, while Joyce and I the middle to allow Alice to drive through," she said.

As the middle began to open up, Alice slowly drove through. As they continued blasting the spiders, Joyce tripped, shot Steven in the chest. While she was lying on the ground, three spiders attacked her as Matthew and Jessica continued shooting until Alice completed her task. Alice jumped out of the SUV and began killing the spiders, allowing Matthew and Jessica to get to the SUV. When they looked back, Joyce had three spiders on top of her.

"We have to help her!" Alice cried.

"There is only one thing that we can do now!" Jessica said.

After Jessica put the car in reverse, Matthew shot Joyce to end her suffering. On the drive to Flagstaff, no one said a word, and Alice sobbed.

An hour later, Jessica drove into her driveway on East Empire Avenue. They got out of the SUV and walked inside her second home.

"Make yourselves at home," she said.

Matthew noticed Jessica's hunting trophies.

"Jessica, did you shoot all these animals?" Matthew asked.

She walked into the room.

"Where's Alice?" she asked.

"She fell asleep on the couch," he said.

"Did you ask about my trophies?" she asked.

"I did, and you must be an excellent shot," he said.

"I received two medals while I served in the Army, one for rifle shooting, and the other pistol shooting," she said.

"Should we talk about what happened in Camp Verde," he asked.

"We did what we had to do," she said. "But I am worried about Alice."

"She took it pretty hard," he said.

Alice walked into the room.

"What's for dinner?" she asked.

"What would you like? There's a Safeway nearby," Jessica said.

"How do spaghetti and meatballs sound?" Matthew asked.

"Sounds great, so let's go shopping!" Alice replied.

When they returned, Matthew made the spaghetti, Jessica the meatballs, and Alice the salad. Afterward, they sat down at the table to enjoy their feast.

"After dinner, let's check on your girlfriend," Jessica said. "Which motel will she choose?"

"Either the Super 8 or Motel 6, off the I40," Alice said. "But I want to talk to you about Joyce."

"I'm sorry for what we had to do," she said.

"I understand!" Alice said. "It's just that I want to thank you for being merciful; I didn't want her to suffer because she was my Mother."

"I'm so sorry, Alice, I didn't know," she said.

We haven't spoken for a while because she didn't like the idea of me being a lesbian," Alice said. "At the hotel, we worked things out, and she wanted to meet Marci."

After dinner, Jessica and Alice drove to the Super 8 motel, but no one named Marci Logan had checked in. They then proceeded to Motel 6. As they parked, Alice saw Marci's car pulling into the parking lot. Alice got out of the SUV and ran to her, where they had a tearful reunion. Marci was sad that she wasn't able to meet Joyce.

"Marci, I want to introduce you to Jessica, the woman who saved my life," Alice said.

"Nice to meet you, Jessica," Marci said.

"Did you have any problems getting here?" Jessica asked.

"It wasn't smooth sailing, but I made it safely," Marci said.

"I have three rooms at my house, so if you two would like to stay until I leave, I'd welcome you, and Matthew can stay in the smaller room," she said.

At the beginning of May, everyone decided to travel to Alaska with Jessica. When they drove into Utah, the temperature was 80 Degrees.

"This higher than normal temperature is concerning," Jessica said. "We may have to live inside my SUV until we get to a colder climate."

"Glad, I brought extra deodorant," Matthew joked.

Everyone laughed.

"Here's how this is going to work," Jessica began. "We will only stop for restroom breaks, gas, supplies, sleep in shifts, and take turns driving to Canada."

"How long will that take?" Alice asked.

"About eighteen hours," Jessica said. "Matthew, you're up."

When they got to the outskirts of Salt Lake City, a group of spiders was attacking a bus full of children. Matthew stopped, and everyone got out with their shotguns. Afterward, the bus driver thanked them.

"Where are you going with these children?" Jessica asked.

"To a protected shelter," he said.

"I think we should follow you there just in case," Matthew said.

When they reached Farmington, Utah, the bus driver turned onto an access road and entered what was once known as The Lagoon Amusement Park, which was surrounded by armed guards. After the children got off the bus, the woman in charge, grilled the bus driver.

"Why were you late, Mr. Smith?" she asked.

"If it weren't for them in the SUV, we wouldn't be here at all," he said. "We were being attacked by spiders when they came to our rescue."

"Were any of the children hurt?"

"Luckily, no," he said.

The woman waved at Jessica to exit her SUV.

"Who are you people?" she asked.

"I am Jessica; this is Matthew, Marci, and Alice," Jessica said.

"That's not what I asked!" she said rudely.

"We're travelers heading to Alaska," Jessica said.

"I think it would best that you get back on the road!" she said rudely.

"If that's the thanks we get for saving those children, you need to take a chill pill," Jessica said rudely. "You're lucky that I don't punch you in the face."

"You wouldn't dare," she said smugly.

She punched her in the stomach instead, and everyone got back into the SUV. As they drove away, one of the armed guards stopped them. Jessica rolled the window down.

"It's about time someone gave her exactly what she needed," he said, laughing.

As they got back on the I15, everyone had a good laugh.

"Some people," Jessica sighed.

"Well, she asked for it," Alice said.

"What a bitch," Marci said.

Fourteen hours later, they crossed into Canada, which was warm. As Marci drove north, it was getting colder. When they arrived in Edmonton, they were finally safe, and they found a motel to sleep.

The next morning, they were on the road again.

Two days later, they arrived in Anchorage, Alaska.

"We're here, but where are we going to live?" Matthew asked.

"A friend of mine left me his house, but it needs work," Jessica said.

"Then let's get to it!" he said.

The work took nearly three months, and both couples married.

One year later, Jessica gave birth to a girl named Joyce in remembrance of Alice's mother and asked Alice and Marci to be her Godparents.

Three years later, she gave birth to Steven.

As they enjoyed their lives, the outside temperature rose because part of the Arctic Circle had been affected when the sun underwent another expansion in 2021. During the same year, the scientific community also discovered that the reason the spiders grew is that one of the great earthquakes ruptured a pocket of unknown gas that spread across the globe.

When Joyce was five years old, and Steven two, they were playing outside when Jessica heard a scream, and she ran out the front door.

"What's wrong, Jelly Bean," Jessica asked.

"I saw a monster," Joyce said.

"Where?" Jessica asked.

"It went over there, behind the trees,"

When Jessica looked, she saw a dark figure moving. She grabbed Joyce and Steven and brought them inside.

"Everyone in the front room now!" Jessica yelled.

"What's wrong?" Alice asked.

"I think our time here is up," she said.

"The spiders are here?" Marci asked.

"Joyce said she saw a monster, so call Matthew on the walkie-talkie, and tell him to get back here pronto," she said.

"Be careful, Jessica," Alice said.

"Also, turn on the warning siren," she said.

As Jessica went outside, Marci turned on the warning siren. Jessica ran in the direction where she saw the dark figure, and then she stopped. As she looked through binoculars, Matthew was running away from several spiders, and then she heard his screams.

When she found Matthew, he had two spiders on top of him, and she shot them. He was in horrible pain as his insides were melting.

"You know what to do," he moaned in pain.

"I love you, Matthew," Jessica cried.

As he looked into her eyes, she ended his suffering, and then she ran back to the house with tears in her eyes. When she went inside, Alice and Marci could tell something was wrong.

"Where's Matthew?" Alice asked.

"They got him," she said sadly.

"I'm sorry, Jessica," Alice said.

They heard military helicopters landing nearby. Everyone in the house went outside. As Jessica wiped away her tears, Army Colonel, Robert Emerson, approached.

"Army Specialist Jessica Langston," he asked.

"Yes, sir!" she said.

"You may dispense with the formalities, Ms. Langston, we need your help," he said.

"What do you need me to do?" she asked.

"The majority of the spiders were killed by other spiders as their food supply dwindled. Approximately three hundred or so remain, and they are heading here," he said. "We need to keep them from entering Anchorage."

"They're already here, and they killed my husband just a few minutes ago," she said.

"Then our Intel was wrong, I'm sorry," he said. "I need you to run a battle line, and I will provide you with the men you need."

"Let's get to it, Colonel!" she said.

Forty men were released into her command, as the colonel left for Anchorage.

"This will be a joint military and civilian operation," she stated. "If any of you men are sharpshooters, please step forward."

Five soldiers stepped up.

"I want you up on my roof, and you may fire when you have a lock on your target," she said. But, aim for their head for a direct kill?"

"Yes, Ma'am!" they said in unison.

The rest of you need to help me dig two shallow canals, ten feet apart," she said.

As they began to dig, the civilians arrived, and everyone worked together. Once the canals were ready, they poured gasoline into them.

"Some of us, including myself, will stand here as bait. I want the rest of you men to divide into teams of two, using a flanking maneuver inside the tree line to the left and right of us to keep our enemy in a manageable position," she said. "When I yell, "Last Stand Alaska," move in, but a word of caution, this enemy will not retreat because of their voracious appetite."

Alice and Marci, please stay inside to protect Joyce and Steven; they already lost their father today," she said. "Those with shotguns, stand next to me, and those with rifles, shoot when you have a clear line of sight!"

An hour later, the spiders appeared. As they approached, the snipers opened fire. Jessica allowed a small group of them to cross the first canal.

"Light 'em up," she ordered.

As the odds stacked against them, she yelled, "Last Stand Alaska."

The soldiers moved in and began shooting. Afterward, they burned the spiders.

The battle against the spiders ended.

As sixty-seven-year-old Jessica sat in her favorite chair telling her grandchildren about the spiders, and the love of her life, Marci and Alice sat on the couch listening.

Two years following her death, the town was renamed Langston Junction in her honor. Marci and Alice gave the eulogy to honor their beloved friend, Jessica.

The End

The Aftermath

DORIAN AND JASON arrived in Hollywood, California, after traveling on foot for six months from British Columbia, searching for their wives. When they arrived at Dorian's house, there was no sign of them.

"Where could they be?" Jason asked.

"Do you think they could make it here after all we've been through?" Dorian asked.

"If anyone has a chance to make it here, they do because we trained them to be more than just survivors," Jason said. "Should we continue to Los Angeles just for the hell of it?"

"Sure, there's nothing for us here at the moment," Dorian said.

They proceeded on to Los Angeles and arrived near MacArthur Park a few hours later.

"I guess we were lucky to survive the nuclear shit storm. It was bad enough when we moved to Canada to avoid the food and water shortage riots, but this day-to-day kill-or-be-killed living environment is taking its toll on me," Jason said.

As they talked, two armed men approached.

"We can take them," Jason whispered.

"We could, but let's see what develops," Dorian whispered back.

"You two come with us," Thomas ordered.

They walked ahead of the two men to where they were going. As they walked through a makeshift compound, they saw women with young children and babies, senior citizens, and a lot of bored teenagers. They were taken into a building and then to a room with a desk. When the colonel walked in, they were surprised.

"Colonel Westin!" they said in unison.

"Knowing your abilities, why did you allow my men to bring you here?" he asked.

"Curiosity," Dorian replied. "But why did they bring us here?"

"They thought you were part of the gang that's been plaguing us," he said. "So, why are you two in Los Angeles?"

"We lost contact with Rachel and Sara after we crashed in Jason's helicopter. He broke his leg in the crash, and we survived in the forest against a pack of wolves. When we finally got to our cabin, they were gone. We checked my house, but there was no sign of them," Dorian said.

"I know how well you two trained your wives, so it's probably just a matter of time before they show," he said. "In the meantime, I need help training my men."

"Okay," Dorian said.

"I'll have Thomas show you where you can bunk," he said.

The next day as Dorian and Jason walked into the colonel's office, the two men who brought them to the compound were sitting at a table.

"This is Thomas and Robert, whom you met yesterday," he said. "Thomas, Robert, this is Dorian and Jason. They served under me in Afghanistan."

"Tell us about this gang problem," Dorian said.

"It started six months ago when they came in and took several women and our food supply. Before they left, they killed two men for trying to stand up against them. Since then, they have been coming once a month to take whatever they want," Thomas said.

"Today, that ends," Jason said. "What weapons do you have?"

"We have all kinds, but we're the only ones who know how to use them," Robert answered.

"That also changes today," Dorian stated. "How many men do you have?"

"Eighteen," Thomas said.

"When do you expect the gang to appear?" Jason asked.

"In two weeks," Thomas replied.

"Gather your men; training starts now," Dorian said.

They began with weapon basics, and by the end of ten days, the men were proficient in their weapon of choice.

Five days later, Robert signaled Dorian that the gang was approaching, and he instructed the men not to shoot the leader. As they approached, he walked outside the compound.

"Who are you?" the leader asked.

"Dorian, and you?" he said.

"I'm Big Dog, so step aside and let us through," he said.

"Are you saying that you are so damned lazy to find a food supply that you have to steal from others?" Dorian asked.

"We control this area, and we take what is ours," he answered.

Dorian stepped back, and then shots rang out.

"Drop your gun, and walk towards me unless you want to die like them," Dorian ordered.

Thomas stood guard as the colonel interrogated Big Dog.

"What are we going to do about their bodies?" Thomas asked.

"Burn them," Dorian said.

Afterward, Dorian and Jason visited the colonel.

"Where's the prisoner?" Jason asked.

"I had to let him go because we don't have anywhere to keep prisoners, and he won't return to his gang unless he wants to die for his failure," he answered.

"Did you get any useful intel from him?" Dorian asked.

"His gang is approximately two hundred strong, and they live in the old militia compound in the Hollywood Hills," he said.

"Since we trained your men, Jason and I will return home to leave a message for the wives, and then we'll return," Dorian said.

"I'll see you then," he said.

On the way back to Hollywood, they stopped at a Walmart for some food supplies. They knew not to stay inside too long because of scavengers, and they went directly to the canned food aisle. They grabbed some soup, spam, and stew and quickly stuffed them inside their backpacks. On their way through the parking lot, someone took a shot at them, and they hid behind a brick storage area, spotting six men.

"What do you want?" Dorian yelled.

"What you took from our store," a man said.

"Then try to take it back from us," Dorian yelled.

They rushed Dorian and Jason, paying with their lives.

"We'd better get moving," Jason warned.

They arrived at Dorian's house four hours later, spray-painted M. Park on the wall, and then sat on the couch to rest. Suddenly, bullets sprayed through the living room window, and they crawled into the bedroom to look outside.

"I see five men," Jason said.

"They must have followed us here from Walmart," Dorian surmised.

They then crawled back into the living room.

"What do you want?" Dorian yelled.

"You killed my brother," Carlos answered.

"I'm sorry, but we didn't have a choice," Dorian said.

"It doesn't matter. I'm still going to kill you," Carlos said.

"Our old tunnel?" Jason asked Dorian.

"Let's go," Dorian said.

They went downstairs to the basement and opened the old tunnel they built connecting their two houses. They then exited out Jason's back door, and around the hedge. They watched the gang open fire again on Dorian's house and waited until they had to reload.

"Drop your guns, or we drop you," Jason warned.

"You killed my brother, and he was the only family I had left," he said.

"I'm sorry," Dorian said.

"I'm sorry too," Carlos said, pointing his pistol.

They had to shoot all five men.

"We'd better get back to the compound," Dorian suggested.

Nine months earlier, Rachel and Sarah were worried since they had lost communication with Dorian and Jason. They hoped that they were alright, but after weeks of waiting, they had to accept the inevitable. They left the cabin as planned on a snowmobile to a cave where they had stored a cache of weapons and a food supply.

While living in the cave, they practiced their fighting skills, exercised heavily, and became lovers. At the end of the fifth month, they returned to the cabin, but there was no sign of their husbands, and they headed south into Washington State.

They arrived at the outskirts of Spokane, Washington, after they had to fight and kill scavengers along the way, but down the road, they spotted three armed guards.

"Why are you blocking the road?" Rachel asked.

"We've been having problems with women disappearing," Mike said.

"Do we look like fucking kidnappers to you?" Rachel asked.

Mike noticed how the women reacted and held their guns, realizing they had military training. He ordered his men to allow them to pass.

"There's a place up ahead called Ma's. Tell her Mike sent you," he said.

They arrived at Ma's and said that Mike sent them. She welcomed them into her old bed and breakfast and showed them to an upstairs room.

"Dinner is at five, so don't be late!" Ma said.

They removed their backpacks and clothing, filled the large bathtub with hot water and bubble bath that Ma provided.

"This feels heavenly," Sarah moaned.

After relaxing in the tub for a time, a bubble fight ensued, and they laughed, which was something they haven't done for a while. After Rachel and Sarah took their bath, they took a nap. Later, as they sat at the dining table, Ma brought in a roast with small potatoes and set the platter on the table. She then went back into the kitchen, brought in some tea, and then she sat down.

"What brings you two to Spokane?" Ma asked.

"We're on our way to Seattle, and then down to Hollywood, California," Rachel said.

"Why there?" Ma asked.

"Hopefully, our husbands will be there," Rachel said.

"Have you heard anything about women vanishing around here?" Ma asked.

"No, why?" Rachel asked.

"Women are vanishing from this area, and no one knows why," Ma said.

"I'm guessing you want our help to find them?" Rachel asked.

"Yes, because you two have specialized training," Ma said.

"Training?" Rachel asked.

"Mike recognized your military training. That's why he sent you to me," Ma said.

"Oh, he did, did he?" Rachel replied angrily.

"Please don't be angry at him. We desperately need your help," Ma said.

Rachel told Ma that they would look into it. When they returned to the room, Sarah was angry.

"What's wrong?" Rachel asked.

"Do we always have to play the hero?" Sarah asked.

"Why do you think Dorian and Jason trained us?" Rachel said. "Besides, it wouldn't be right to abandon those women when we have the training."

"I'm sorry, Rachel! It's just that I'm so tired of all this fighting and killing," Sarah said.

"I don't like it either, but I'm willing to do whatever it takes to survive with the person I love," Rachel said.

"I love you too," Sarah said.

They fell asleep in each other's arms.

The next morning Rachel looked at a map while Sarah slept. She circled the areas where Ma said the women had vanished, and then she remembered the militia compound twenty miles from there, and she woke Sarah.

"What is it, Rachel?" Sarah asked.

"I think I found the missing women!" Rachel announced.

"You woke me to tell me a theory?" Sarah yelled.

"It's not a theory, Sarah!" Rachel stated. "There's a militia compound nearby, and it's central to the women's disappearances."

Rachel went downstairs for coffee and told Ma, where the women could be.

"Before the apocalypse, my husband and I kept tabs on militia groups in case something like this ever happened, but most were much too radical for us. This morning, I remembered there's a militia compound twenty miles from here," Rachel explained.

"Why aren't I aware of it?" Ma asked.

"Because they're highly secretive," Rachel said.

When Rachel walked into the room, Sarah greeted her with a hug.

I'm sorry about this morning, but I haven't slept this good in a long time," Sarah said. "When do we rescue the women?"

"We leave at first light tomorrow," Rachel answered.

The next afternoon, they arrived outside the hills where the militia compound is hidden. After hiking up and down several hills, they called it quits, and set up camp.

Around 10:00 pm, they heard a woman scream. They quickly walked up and down two more hills when they saw the compound below. They watched as two men dragged a woman kicking and screaming into a small hut.

"I'm going to kill those fuckers!" Sarah said.

"You'll get your chance," Rachel said

Sarah passed the time by pushing and pulling her knife in and out of the ground.

Two hours later, they crawled beneath the compound fence. Sarah found the first guard and stabbed him several times because he was one of the men who raped the woman. They killed four sentries in all, found a set of keys, and then went to the long building to unlock the door.

"Who are you?" Mary asked.

"Your rescue party. How many women are in here?" Rachel asked.

"About sixty! Who else is with you?" Mary asked.

"We're it!" Sarah said.

"You two against fifty men?" Mary exclaimed.

"Where's does the commander live?" Rachel asked.

"In the house at the back of the compound," Mary replied. "How did you get past the guards?"

"We didn't!" Sarah said.

Mary saw the blood on Sarah and knew they meant business.

"Do they have an armory?" Rachel asked.

"It's next to the commander's house, but he has the only key," Mary answered.

"Mary, you come with me," Rachel said.

Sarah stayed behind to protect the women while Rachel and Mary went to the commander's house. After Rachel crawled through an open window, she slowly crept into the commander's bedroom. She found a young girl chained to his bed, and she looked at Rachel through swollen eyes and a bruised face. Rachel got angry and punched the commander hard in the throat, and then stabbed him. She found his keys and freed the girl, who rushed into her arms.

"Wait here until I come back," Rachel promised.

Rachel crawled back out the window.

"To the armory," she told Mary.

When they opened the armory, they found a cache of weapons. They filled a duffle bag full of knives and gave one to each woman. As the men slept, the women crept inside their barracks and killed them one by one. Afterward, they went back to their building to sleep. Rachel and Sarah slept in the commander's guest room, with the girl named Beth in the middle.

In the morning, Rachel, Sarah, and Beth walked outside. Rachel told the women to find fuel and stack the dead in the courtyard. After they finished the task, Rachel addressed them.

"Today you stand victorious over your captors, and it's time to send them to hell for what they have done here. Pour the fuel upon the pyre and let it burn," Rachel said.

Two hours later, they gathered around Rachel again.

"Those of you who have family in Spokane may return home, and those who haven't may stay here with us," Rachel announced.

After five women left the compound to tell Ma everything, Rachel and Sarah decided to raise Beth as their own. Rachel then addressed the women who stayed behind.

"We shall make this place our home and become as one. Sarah and I will train you to become fierce warriors like the Amazons of old," Rachel stated. "From this day, we will be known as the 'Order of the Hawk' so tonight we feast, but tomorrow, we train!"

Dorian and Jason were training their men in hand-to-hand combat when a stranger appeared in the compound. They took him to the colonel for questioning.

"Who are you?" Dorian asked.

"The name is Miller," he answered.

"Why are you here?" the colonel asked.

"I need protection from the gang," Miller said.

"Why would they be after you?" Dorian asked.

"They wanted to use my explosive expertise to destroy your compound, but I refused, and they locked me up," Miller explained.

"Maybe you're their spy," Dorian stated.

"You're right, I wouldn't believe me either, but I can prove it by giving you something they don't have," Miller said.

"And what would that be?" Dorian asked.

"A food supply," Miller answered.

"Where?" Dorian asked.

"Before I say anything, I want your assurance that I'll be protected!" Miller said.

"If you are telling the truth, you have it," the colonel offered.

"At Long Beach Harbor, there are several shipping containers filled with food items. I know because I worked there as their Explosive Safety Officer," Miller said.

"Dorian, take him and three men with you to find those containers," the colonel said.

"But...!" Miller said.

"No, buts, Miller! You're coming with us," Dorian said. "I'm going to check your story, and for your sake, you'd better not be lying."

They began their two-day walk to Long Beach. When they arrived, they got into a firefight with a group of scavengers. After Dorian's men gathered the dead men's ammo, Miller led them to the containers. Dorian was shocked to see bags of rice, beans, flour, sugar, tea, etc. He removed Miller's handcuffs and apologized for not believing him.

"We need to get this food back to the compound," Dorian said.

"There are two quads with trailers in that container over there," Miller pointed.

They loaded the trailers with as much food as they could carry and rode to the compound. They arrived with Miller in the front, and everyone cheered.

Aiguo Zhang grew up in a boys' home after his parents died in the revolution of 1947 when the Republic of China adopted its constitution. Seventy-two years later, he was now the highest-ranking admiral, but a hatred burned inside of him for what China did to his parents.

During the past five years, he has had ten decommissioned aircraft carriers and two supply ships refurbished to house eighty-thousand men. He has also had nutritionists working on developing a new superfood to eliminate the need for the vast amount of supplies to sustain his men. The superfood is called 'black rice' in the shape of a ball that provides each man their daily nutritional requirements, eliminating the need for eating three meals a day.

His ships were fully operational and ready for launch. As a helicopter flew him to his ship, Yang Liu, he gave orders to get underway. As his vessels moved through the ocean, China was unaware of his actual destination. On the very next day, his dying friend sent a signal to the computer chips he had secretly reprogrammed for nuclear launch systems around the world. In less than a day, the civilized world, including China, ceased to exist. Since his ships were in the middle of the ocean, his men were unaware.

It took twenty days for ten Chinese Ships to reach Long Beach Harbor, and eighteen days for one to arrive at Seattle.

As Dorian and his men loaded food supplies onto the trailers, a second time, he spotted the ships entering the harbor. As he peered through his binoculars, he saw a Chinese flag.

"Why are the Chinese here?" Dorian asked.

After the Chinese spotted them, the ships began shelling the harbor.

"Move," Dorian yelled.

They left just in time, as a shell landed near the food containers. After they arrived safely back at the compound, Dorian hurried to the colonel.

"What's wrong, Dorian?" he asked.

"We're under attack!" Dorian stated.

"By whom?" he asked.

"After we loaded the supplies, Chinese Ships began shelling the harbor," Dorian replied.

"Let's get everyone to the tunnels," he said.

The tunnels proved to be the perfect hiding spot when the Chinese appeared. Dorian, Jason, and their men went on nightly recons to see what they were up to, but they couldn't come up with any logical explanation. Afterward, the gang was rounded up by the Chinese and executed. The survivors realized that they were at war with the Chinese.

A month crawled by in the tunnels as their food supply dwindled. Dorian and Jason met with the colonel to discuss the problem.

"What did you two want to discuss?" the colonel asked.

"Our food supplies are running dangerously low, and our men can't search for supplies if we want to keep the tunnels safe," Dorian said.

"What are you proposing?" he asked.

"To train the older boys to carry their weight around here," Dorian responded.

"To do what, exactly?" he asked.

"To find food wherever they can," Dorian answered.

"But, they're children!" he exclaimed.

"I would never propose such a thing unless it was necessary for our survival," Dorian said.

"I hoped it wouldn't come down to this, but you're right," he said.

"I'm sorry, Colonel, but these are unusual times," Dorian said.

The colonel left as Thomas and Robert walked up.

"We will start training the older boys to search for supplies. Thomas, I'm appointing you to be their trainer," Dorian said.

"What kind of training?" Thomas asked.

"Getting inside the Chinese encampments and being able to defend themselves, if necessary," Dorian replied.

"You expect them to kill Chinese soldiers?" Thomas asked.

"If it comes to that, yes," Dorian replied.

"How much time do I have to train them?" Thomas asked.

"In three weeks, our supplies will be exhausted," Dorian answered.

"I'll do my best," Thomas promised.

Two weeks later, Thomas addressed the boys.

"You boys have impressed me by how quickly you've learned your new skills," Thomas said. "Our first mission will be at the militia compound up in the Hollywood Hills."

Clancy walked up to Thomas.

"The guys are a bit nervous, Thomas," Clancy said.

"Let's see if we can take their minds off the mission," Thomas suggested.

He turned to the other boys.

"I think we should name our band of misfits," Thomas joked.

After they suggested various names, Clancy threw one out.

"How about the Wolf Pack?" he suggested.

Everyone liked it.

Two hours later, Thomas and the Wolf Pack arrived at the old militia compound now occupied by the Chinese.

"Thomas, do you hear that?" Clancy whispered.

"It sounds like crying," Thomas said.

"In that shed over there," Jake pointed.

"I'll check it out while you boys do what you came to do," Thomas said.

The boys went to work picking up bags of rice and stuffing them inside their packs while the guard slept. Thomas opened the shed, finding several women inside.

"Who are you?" Athena asked.

"My name is Thomas, and one of my men is waiting outside the fence.

"Where are we going?" Athena asked.

"To the tunnels in Los Angeles," he said.

They followed him to the fence, where Clancy was waiting.

"Follow Clancy, and he'll take you to safety," he assured them.

The alarm suddenly sounded as the last boy crawled under the fence.

"Get them out of here, Clancy!" Thomas commanded.

"I'm not leaving without you, Thomas," Clancy said.

"Get everyone to safety Clancy, that's an order!" Thomas said.

He hesitated, and then he led the women away. When he looked back, Thomas got shot, and he fell to his knees, but Athena grabbed him, and they left the area.

The Wolf Pack returned with supplies and the women.

"Where's Thomas?" Dorian asked.

"He didn't make it," Clancy replied tearfully.

"What happened?" Dorian asked.

"The alarm sounded, and he stayed behind to create a diversion," Clancy explained.

"I'm sorry, Clancy," Dorian said.

"He was like...a father...to me," Clancy said sobbing.

"Go rest while I talk to the women," Dorian said.

"Why were you being held captive?" Dorian asked.

"They used us as cooks and sex slaves," Athena said.

"I'm sorry, but would you be able to tell me about your captors?" Dorian asked.

"I overheard Captain Chen speaking to Admiral Zhang in English on the radio," she said. "From what I understood, the admiral is trying to make Los Angeles his dynasty."

"Jeffries will take you to a place where you can rest," Dorian said.

Jason walked up to Dorian.

"Get any intel?" Jason asked.

"Athena told me that the Chinese intend to make Los Angeles their home. We need to find a way to dissuade them even though we're outnumbered and outgunned," he said.

They told the colonel.

The next morning, they discussed the previous night's mission.

"I'm stunned by the loss of Thomas," the colonel said.

"He did what he thought best to save everyone," Dorian said.

"I think Clancy should replace him," the colonel suggested.

"He's young, but he's a good fit," Dorian agreed.

They called Clancy into the meeting.

"We've been discussing what you did last night. You followed orders, and we know leaving Thomas behind wasn't easy for you," the colonel said.

"How would you like to lead the Wolf Pack?" Dorian asked.

"You think I could handle the job?" Clancy asked.

"Go tell the Wolf Pack they have a new leader," the colonel said.

The Hawk compound had become a well-oiled machine as the women trained in various weapons, hand-to-hand combat, and strengthening exercises to transform themselves into physically capable warriors. Rachel called a meeting to determine if it was time to leave the compound. They unanimously voted to head to Seattle.

It took the Hawks a month to get to the outskirts of Seattle. Rachel signaled them to stop as she saw something she didn't like through her binoculars.

"I need to take a closer look," Rachel advised.

She used the brush and trees as cover to get closer, and she saw Chinese soldiers.

"What the fuck are they doing in Seattle?" she wondered.

As she watched, two Chinese soldiers were executing people.

"Fuck!" Rachel said.

She saw several women and a child waiting their turn, and she moved in closer. She let the first arrow fly, then the second, killing two Chinese soldiers. She pulled her arrows from the dead and told the women to follow her.

"Who are these women?" Sarah asked.

"POW's," Rachel said. "The Chinese have invaded Seattle."

"Why would they be in Seattle?" Sarah asked.

"Hopefully, someone here can answer that question, but it's not safe here since I killed two soldiers to save them. We'll retreat to the old school we passed earlier," Rachel said.

The Hawks went to the abandoned school they spotted earlier off the main road. Rachel asked Beth to get the Hawks situated in the gym while she talked to the women.

"Do any of you have a clue about what's going on in Seattle?" Rachel asked.

"After the Chinese arrived, they began executing survivors, but that's all we know," Amanda said. "So, who are you, people?"

"We're the Order of the Hawk," Rachel said. "Today, you may rest, but tomorrow you will be assigned duties to earn your place with us."

Rachel went to address the Hawks.

"As you are aware, these are troubled times, and what I am about to tell you is difficult. For some unknown reason, the Chinese have arrived in Seattle, and they're executing Americans. So, let's gather in the circle of fire to decide our fate," Rachel said.

Everyone voted to fight.

"I want you to pair off because we're going into Seattle to wreak havoc upon our enemy," Rachel said. "This is what you've been training to do, and you must kill without mercy."

She returned to the POWs.

"We will return late tomorrow, and a meal must be ready for us," Rachel said.

At 7:00 a.m., the Hawks entered Seattle. By the end of the day, they killed more than a hundred soldiers. She left two Hawks behind to keep watch. A meal was waiting for them when they got back to their hideout.

"Thank you, Amanda," Rachel said.

"You're welcome, but I have a request," Amanda replied. "I want to become a Hawk."

"Do you know how to fight?" Rachel asked.

"I know a few things," Amanda answered.

"In the gym in one hour," Rachel ordered.

Someone handed Amanda a broom handle as she entered the gym.

"To join us, you must get through the gauntlet," Rachel said.

Amanda fought valiantly and made it through, but not without bruises.

The next morning, the Hawks, Rachel left behind, returned with some news.

"The Chinese are killing everyone they find, including children," Lisa reported.

"Sadly, this is war, and collateral damage will occur," Rachel responded.

"What are we going to do?" Lisa asked.

"Hit them hard and fast to divert their attention from other survivors," Rachel said.

"When do we go back in?" Lisa asked.

"In two days," Rachel promised.

A month had passed, and the Hawks had killed more than twenty-five percent of Admiral Han's army. His army was no match against the Hawks stealth tactics.

As the colonel's men continued their nightly recons, everyone took a turn, including himself, but, one night, he and Wilson didn't return. Dorian and Jason went to find them. They used the hidden entrance in their old compound and saw the colonel tied to the flag pole, but there was no sign of Wilson. They crawled in close to whisper, while they hid in the shadows.

"Colonel!" Dorian whispered.

"Dorian?" he whispered.

"Yes," Dorian replied. "Where's Wilson?"

"Dead," he answered in pain.

"What happened?" Dorian asked.

"We have a traitor amongst us," he explained.

"Who?" Dorian asked.

"Hunt," he answered.

"I'll fix that leak," Dorian said.

"Dorian, you must take over for me," he said.

"We're here to rescue you, Colonel," Dorian said.

"I can't leave because they broke my legs," he said.

"I'm sorry, Colonel," Dorian said.

"Don't be. I had a good run," the colonel said.

Dorian saw two Chinese soldiers and a captain approaching the colonel.

"Get the hell out of here," he insisted.

Dorian and Jason left the compound as the captain questioned the colonel.

"Where are your people?" Captain Chen asked.

"What people?" he asked.

Captain Chen kicked one of his broken legs, causing him to cry out in pain.

"The ones your friend told me about after we spared his miserable life," Captain Chen said.

"Fuck you!" he said.

Dorian and Jason heard a shot, and they knew what it meant. On their way back to the tunnels, two Chinese soldiers chased after them. As Dorian and Jason ran, Dorian almost fell into a pit that wasn't there earlier, but the soldiers weren't so lucky. As they tried to climb out, something grabbed one of them, and they heard his blood-curdling screams. The second soldier tried desperately to get out, but his screams began soon after.

"What the fuck just happened?" Dorian said.

"I don't know, but there's something large down there," Jason replied.

Dorian told the survivors about the colonel.

The next day, Dorian and Jason had a quick meeting with their men.

"We don't have a chance in hell against the Chinese, but we can at least take as many as we can with us," Dorian said.

After the meeting, Dorian went to talk to the women. He told them what they were about to do, and he asked them to be a cook and confidant for a man of their choosing. They agreed, and Athena chose Dorian. The next day, he and Hunt went on one last recon before beginning their new mission. As Dorian approached the pit, he went around it. In time, Hunt made his move. As Dorian rolled to his right, Hunt fell into the hole.

"Looks like the shoe is on the other foot, Hunt!" Dorian said.

"If you get me out of here, I'll tell you everything," he said.

"You were responsible for the death of Johnson, Wilson, and the colonel," Dorian said.

Hunt heard growling, and he saw two large eyes coming at him.

"Something is down here," he said.

"It's called justice," Dorian replied.

As he walked away, Hunt screamed. When he returned, Athena had dinner waiting.

The Hawks suffered two losses during their last battle, but the Chinese losses were far more significant. With over seventy percent of his soldier's dead, Admiral Han realized he was fighting a losing battle. He sent a messenger to his enemy and invited them to meet with him. Rachel was skeptical but met with him anyway.

"Why did you invade Seattle?" she asked.

"Since the U.S. is a wasteland, China decided to make Seattle and Los Angeles settlements for our people," he said.

"You don't know, do you?" she asked.

"Know what?" he asked.

"That nukes also destroyed China," she answered.

"My Friend, Admiral Zhang, would have told me if that were true," he said.

"I'll give you one hour to learn the truth," she said.

After he returned, he wouldn't look Rachel in the face.

"He has known since we left China, and I'm ashamed for what I have done. My men will be returning to China today," he said.

After he killed himself, his men walked away. Rachel returned with the news.

"It's not the time to rejoice because they need us in Los Angeles," she said.

After the Hawks watched the Chinese ship leave the harbor, they began their trek south.

Dorian and Jason's men continued their mission, and the Wolf Pack theirs.

As time passed, Dorian and Jason accepted the loss of Rachel and Sarah, but only Dorian moved on as he and Athena became a couple.

Miller, the resident explosives expert, was working on chemical bottle grenades similar to Molotov cocktails but would emit poisonous gas. Dorian and Jason were planning to use them in a series of blitzkrieg attacks against the Chinese.

The next night, they divided into teams of two to cover the nine Chinese camps. Each tossed bottle grenades into the Chinese sleeping quarters, killing scores of men. The next night, they attacked again, forcing Captain Chen to break radio silence to contact Admiral Zhang for replacements.

"Captain, I just picked up some Chinese chatter, but the signal originated off the coast of California," Mister Elway reported.

"Are you certain, Mister Elway?" Captain Wilburton asked.

"Yes, sir. I checked three times. Captain Chen was talking to Admiral Zhang about replacing his men after chemical weapons killed them."

"Ensign Carlton, what's the latest global radiation readings?" he asked.

"Negligible, Sir," Ensign Carlton responded.

"We've been down here long enough," he said.

The submarine crew of the Titan had been living in an experimental city below the polar ice cap. They had remained there because of the nuclear apocalypse. They evacuated and boarded the U.S.S. Titan, a Jupiter-class submarine.

"All ahead at half speed, Ensign Johnson," he ordered.

"Aye, Captain!" the Ensign replied. "Heading, Sir?"

"33 Degrees North, 118 Degrees West-Long Beach, California," he said.

Captain Chen received his replacements and additional processing units for producing the black rice. Dorian and Jason noticed a strange device after killing a guard.

"I wonder what these things make," Jason pondered.

"What's under those tarps over there?" Dorian asked.

As they explored, Dorian found black rice in a sealed container and opened it. He picked up the strange looking ball of rice and smelled it.

"Smells good," he said before he took a bite. "And it tastes good."

Jason tried one as well.

A few minutes later, they felt energized.

"Fuck!" he said.

"What's wrong?" Jason asked.

"These are why we have never seen Chinese soldiers eating," he said.

They destroyed the unit.

As the Hawks moved south towards Los Angeles, they picked up additional women, making them seventy strong. Rachel and Sarah's adopted daughter, Beth, had blossomed into a beautiful young woman as she turned eighteen. They loved her, and she loved them, but she yearned for a different kind of love. Rachel and Sarah talked to her about sex, even though she knew what it was about after being raped. They explained their marriages and how they ended up together.

Dorian and Jason destroyed several Chinese food processing units, but new ones quickly replaced them.

"The five processing units we destroyed were replaced. Does anyone have any ideas about what we should do next?" Dorian asked.

"If we destroy more units, we can see where the replacements come from," Jeffries said.

"Great idea," Dorian said. "So, I need two volunteers to go to Long Beach."

The volunteers discovered that the units came from one ship, and the food from another.

"We need to put that supply ship out of commission," Dorian said.

"We need a boat, and explosives," Jason said.

"I'm sure Miller could whip something up," Dorian replied. "And I know where there's a rubber raft."

"That would take us two hours to row that far out into the harbor," Jason said.

"I know it will be difficult. That's why it's a three-man operation," Dorian said.

"What would the third person do?" Jason asked.

"Drop the explosive inside the ship's cargo hold," Dorian said.

They found Miller and told him what they needed.

"Rice dust is highly volatile, so you only need a spark," Miller said.

A few days later, Clancy volunteered.

They approached the ship late at night. After Clancy climbed up the anchor chain, he noticed that no one was guarding the ship. He found the cargo hold and tossed in a small explosive device. As he began his climb down the anchor chain, the ship unexpectedly exploded. Dorian and Jason assumed the worse, and then there was a tug on the raft.

"We thought we lost you," Dorian said.

"I wasn't expecting that kind of explosion," Clancy replied.

"I didn't think we would sink a ship, but we did," Jason said.

The Chinese lost their entire food supply.

"Captain! There's more Chinese chatter. Someone blew up their supply ship," Mister Elway reported.

"What the hell is going on in Long Beach?" the Captain asked. "Mister Elway, keep me posted."

"Aye, Captain," Mister Elway said.

The survivors were now in competition with the Chinese for food supplies, and their only option was to go back to Long Beach to see if any of the food containers survived the Chinese shelling. Dorian, Jason, and Jeffries traveled at night to get there. When they got to Long Beach, the harbor was a disaster. Fortunately, they were able to navigate around the wreckage to find the food containers still intact. They determined it would be impossible to bring it back to the tunnels, but Dorian had another idea. He remembered the Jergins Tunnel and how it's connected to a hotel. It would be perfect for the survivors to hide since the Chinese always traveled straight to Los Angeles from the harbor. They found the tunnel and checked the hotel. It was relatively close to the food containers.

After they returned to Los Angeles, they told everyone that they were moving to Long Beach. It took them a few days, but everyone arrived safely. Dorian said goodbye to Athena as he headed back to Los Angeles with his men.

When they returned, two Chinese soldiers were guarding the entrance.

"Damn it! They must have Miller," Jason said.

"I hope he finished the arrows," Dorian said. "Let's check our hiding place."

They opened the trunk of a burned-out car, and the arrows were in there.

"Miller is an important asset, and we can't afford to lose him," Dorian said.

They found Miller tied to the same flagpole as the colonel. When they got closer, it wasn't Miller, but a Chinese soldier. The compound lit up, and Chinese soldiers scurried. Dorian and Jason used the arrows, causing explosions amid the chaos. They destroyed several makeshift buildings that had been constructed by the Chinese. As they got to their secret entrance, Jason was shot by Captain Chen in the back. Dorian picked him up and carried him away. As they rejoined their men, they went to Dorian's house. Jason had lost a lot of blood.

"I'm sorry, Dorian," Jason said.

"Just hang in there, Jason," Dorian said.

"Tell Sarah that I love her. Will you do that for me?" Jason said.

He gasped his last breath, and Dorian began CPR, but it was no use.

"He's gone, Dorian," Jeffries said.

"I can revive him," Dorian insisted.

"Dorian! We'll take it from here," Jeffries said.

They dug a grave in the back of Jason's house and placed Jason inside.

"We must accept the fact that we all may die in this war, but I'm not going down without a fight. I lost my best friend today, and I need some ideas as to how we can take out as many of those Chinese bastards, as we can" Dorian said.

"What about suicide runs?" Jeffries suggested. "We divide into teams and run straight at them, and shoot as many as we can."

They laughed because it was such an absurd idea that it might work. Suddenly there was a noise at the front door, and everyone jumped when Clancy walked in.

"What are you doing here, Clancy?" Dorian asked.

"We came to help," he responded. "Where's Jason?"

"We buried him out back," Jeffries answered.

"I'm sorry, Dorian," he said sadly.

Dorian explained what they were about to do.

"Our trial run will be at the militia compound where Thomas died," Dorian said.

The next morning, they discovered that the compound wasn't well guarded. Dorian spotted a lookout in the wooden tower and fired an explosive arrow. The guard fell to his death after the tower exploded. As Chinese soldiers scrambled, the teams ran through the camp shooting every soldier in sight. They caught the Chinese off-guard because they weren't expecting an assault. Afterward, they opened the armory to find a cache of assault rifles and ammo. They also found some MRE's, and each man ate two. They slept peacefully for a change.

For a month, their suicide campaigns worked, killing over a thousand Chinese soldiers, but their replacements were never-ending. Dorian and his men were hiding in the South part of Los Angeles as the Hawks arrived at the northern outskirts. The Chinese had no clue they had to contend with another enemy.

The Hawks went straight to work, killing Chinese Soldiers as Dorian and his men continued their efforts, but neither group knew about the other. Captain Chen was beginning to worry because he knew about Dorian and his men, but not the other unseen force. The Hawks were like ghosts using Ninja stealth techniques. In their first week, they took over an encampment, making it their base of operations, which they defended with precision.

"Captain! I picked up some more Chinese chatter. It appears that someone else is giving them hell," Ensign Elway reported.

"How far are we from Long Beach?" the captain asked.

"A week away, Captain," Ensign Johnson replied.

"Let's crank her up. There are Americans who need our help," the captain said.

"Aye, Captain!" Ensign Johnson said.

The Hawks continued their rampage against the Chinese as

Dorian, and his men did what they could. On a Hawk excursion, Dorian caught sight of one and followed her to their encampment. He was shocked to see nothing but warrior women. Dorian knew they were both fighting against the Chinese, but who were they? Two Hawks captured Dorian and took him to their leader.

"Rachel?" he asked.

She hugged him, and then she quickly backed away.

"I was wondering if you were alive. Where's Jason?" she asked.

"He died after trying to rescue one of our men," he replied.

Sarah walked in and hugged him.

"Where's Jason?" Sarah asked.

"He's dead," he said.

"How?" Sarah asked.

"Trying to save one of our men," he answered.

"Where is he buried?" Sarah asked.

"In his backyard," Dorian said.

"Were you with him when it happened?" Sarah asked.

"He died in my arms," he said sadly. "He asked me to tell you that he loved you."

"I loved him too," Sarah said. "But, I wish he were here so I could tell him that things are different now in person."

"Is there something you two are trying to say?" he asked.

"You know that I have always loved you, but I'm with someone else now," Rachel said.

"I knew you two would find each other someday," he said.

"You knew?" Rachel asked.

"The way you two always looked at each other, it wasn't difficult to figure out," he said.

"So, you're alright with us being together?" Rachel asked.

Just then, Beth walked in.

"Hi, Moms," Beth said.

"Moms?" Dorian asked.

"This is our adopted daughter, Beth," Sarah explained.

"Who's the dude?" Beth asked.

"Dorian," Rachel said.

"I've heard a lot about you," Beth said.

He didn't know how to respond.

"I've been wondering why the Chinese were so busy with the north camps," he said.

"We've been giving them hell, but they seem to multiply," Rachel said.

"That's because soldiers from the ships are replacing them," he said.

"How many ships?" Rachel asked.

"They had ten, but we blew up their food supply ship," he said.

"How many men do you have left?" Rachel asked.

"Thirty," Dorian said.

"With us, that's a hundred," Rachel said. "So, you need to bring your people here so we can protect them."

"They're already safe, and my girlfriend is about ready to give birth," he said.

"What's her name?" Rachel asked.

"Athena," he replied.

"Then I will send some of my Hawks to protect them," Rachel said.

She sent ten Hawks with Dorian. On their way to Long Beach, they ran into Chinese soldiers, but the Hawks took them out with precision.

Two days later, everyone was ecstatic to see Dorian. However, they wondered about the female warriors.

"Who are they?" Athena asked.

"They're Rachel's warriors," he answered.

"Rachel is alive?" Athena asked.

"And so is Sarah," he said.

"Does Rachel know about us?" Athena asked.

"She does, and she and Sarah have an adopted daughter named Beth," he said. "That's her over there."

The American military had regrouped in the Midwest, led by General Tom Sheridan. He declared martial law until the government was up and running. Their mission—to restore law and order. Currently, they are two-hundred thousand strong and divided into two groups. General Mason Phillips is leading the West Coast force and is two weeks out from Los Angeles, unaware of the Chinese.

"Captain! I just picked up some American military chatter," Mister Elway said.

"Is there any way for us to contact them?" he asked.

"Only by shortwave radio, and hopefully someone is listening," Mister Elway answered.

"Make it so, Mister Elway," he ordered.

"Aye, Captain!" Mister, Elway replied.

For two hours, he tried contacting them, but no one answered.

After Dorian and his men returned to the Hawk compound, he met with Rachel and Sarah to discuss future raids. A few minutes into the meeting, they were interrupted by Beth.

"There's a group of Chinese soldiers coming our way," she announced.

"Tell everyone to get into battle positions," Rachel said.

Everyone prepared for battle. The Chinese didn't know there was a group of Hawks hidden outside their compound, waiting for them.

As the Chinese arrived, arrows flew, killing dozens of them. Then a firefight began. The Chinese threw several grenades into the compound, injuring three Hawks, including Beth. The order was given for the Hawks to attack from the rear, led by Amanda. After the brief battle, Rachel, Dorian, and Sarah tended to the wounded as the others stacked the dead soldiers to burn them. Luckily, a piece of shrapnel only grazed Beth.

"God damned Chinese!" Sarah yelled.

"It's only a flesh wound, and Beth will be fine," Rachel assured her.

"I think we should be taking the fight to them instead of letting them come here," Sarah said.

"You're right," Rachel said. "They know where we are, and it will be only a matter of time before they send more soldiers."

"What do you propose we do, Rachel?" Dorian asked.

"To run at them from four sides since they won't be expecting us tomorrow. We will divide and conquer," Rachel said.

"We will attack from the south, and you can cover the other three sides," Dorian said. "We will leave in the next hour so we can get below the southern Chinese encampment."

During the next few days, the Hawks, Dorian, and his men gave the Chinese hell causing substantial loses. Captain Chen was once again forced to break radio silence and called Admiral Zhang. More soldiers arrived in Los Angeles.

"Captain! The Chinese are sending additional soldiers to Los Angeles. It seems the Americans are giving them hell," Mister Elway said.

"How far are we from Long Beach?" he asked.

"We arrive tomorrow, Captain," Mister Elway replied.

"Try contacting the American military again," he ordered.

"Aye, Captain," Mister Elway replied.

An hour later, Mister Elway finally contacted someone at the other end.

"Who am I speaking with?" Captain Rogers asked.

"This is Ensign Elway from the U.S.S. Titan. My captain needs to speak to your commanding officer straight away," Mister Elway responded.

The two commanders spoke. General Phillips was caught off-guard about the Chinese.

As Dorian, his men, and the Hawks continued their raids; the U.S.S. Titan arrived in Long Beach harbor, where they saw nine Chinese ships.

"It's time for a little payback," the Captain said. "Ready torpedoes!"

"Aye, Captain!" Mister Elway said.

Mister Elway relayed the command to the launch bay.

"Fire tubes 1 through 4," the Captain ordered.

The torpedoes took only a few seconds to hit two Chinese ships.

The Chinese ground forces began retreating to Long Beach, but Captain Chen and his men stayed behind. As the Hawks moved south, they ran into his soldiers. There were too many of them, so the Hawks were forced to retreat after losing four. Amanda was one, and later her daughter cried in Sarah's arms.

The U.S.S. Titan sank three additional Chinese ships. Two ships tried to make a run for it, but the submarine sunk them as well, leaving two Chinese vessels in the harbor.

The battles stopped, and the Hawks returned to their encampment. Captain Chen received a strange communiqué from Admiral Han's ship. He learned that Admiral Zhang has been lying to him and his men about China.

The next day, General Phillips arrived outside the Hawk encampment and was surprised by the female warriors. He asked to speak to their leader, who was Rachel. She explained everything about Seattle and their exploits in Los Angeles. Rachel asked about the explosions, and General Phillips told her about the U.S.S. Titan keeping the Chinese from leaving Long Beach harbor. Dorian and his men headed back to the Hawk compound and were happy to see the U.S. Military. He asked to speak to their commanding officer.

"What the hell are you doing here, Dorian?" General Phillips asked.

"Been fighting the Chinese ever since they arrived," he answered.

"Your fight is over now," General Phillips said. "Where's Jason?"

"He was killed by Captain Chen. He's the one leading the Chinese ground forces," he replied.

"I'm sorry about Colonel Westin, I know he was your friend," General Phillips said.

"He also died at the hands of Captain Chen," Dorian said. "And I'm going to kill him when I find him, so my fight isn't quite over."

Sarah overheard the conversation and went looking for Captain Chen.

Captain Chen killed Admiral Zhang, and he told the men that he had committed suicide. Captain Chen was angry about losing his men to the Hawks and Dorian's men and ordered a full ground assault. He didn't know that U.S. Military forces were heading his way. General Phillips divided his army in half. One half headed straight to Long Beach Harbor from the north, while the other half went southeast with the Hawks and Dorian's men.

Captain Chen encountered General Phillips' Army and took on heavy casualties and even more when the southeast division entered from the side. The Chinese surrendered.

General Phillips ordered Captain Chen to leave and never return.

"Wait!" Dorian said. "Captain Chen and I have some unfinished business."

The two men fought an epic sword battle. As Dorian fell backward, Captain Chen quickly took advantage, but Dorian rolled to his side and got back up on his feet. They battled for their lives until Captain Chen gained momentum. Captain Chen tried to strike a fatal blow, but Dorian blocked it, receiving a gash and a broken forearm. He fought bravely with his remaining hand but was losing to his trained adversary. As Dorian fell, Captain Chen prepared to thrust his sword into him when an arrow pierced his heart. Dorian saw that Sarah fired the arrow, ending the war in Los Angeles.

Dorian was grateful to Sarah because he was about to become a father. Rachel and Sarah adopted Amanda's daughter as their own, just as they did with Beth. Two weeks later, the Hawks returned to Washington State without Beth to their old compound. Dorian became a father and named his son Jason after his best friend, and he became the mayor of Los Angeles. Clancy was appointed to Washington D.C. as a Delegate to help reestablish the United States Government, and then he and Beth married. At the bottom of the pit, two large overweight Bengal Tigers were found and shot.

The End

The Gold Three-Head Chain

WHILE GEORGE MATHEWS vacationed in Jamaica, he found the usual souvenirs until he came across a booth with an older woman sitting on an old stool. Although her offerings were limited, they were unique, and he looked at an odd-looking chain with three gold heads. When he picked it up, it vibrated in his hand. He asked her how much it was, and she gave it to him as a gift. As he walked away with his prize, she smiled.

A week later, he returned to work, and at the end of the day, he was exhausted, which was unusual for him being twenty-five years old.

After a few days of feeling tired, he decided to see a doctor.

The doctor did a complete physical and ordered several bloodwork panels. A week later, he received a call from the doctor asking him to verify his age.

"Based on your test results, I would have guessed you to be in your forties," Dr. Barnes said. "You must be living a very stressful life."

George made an appointment with another doctor for a second opinion, and that doctor told him the same thing. Afterward, he went to Starbucks, where five old Jamaican men pointed at him. After he got his order, he went outside to confront them.

"Why were you pointing at me?" he snarled.

They pointed to his chain with the three gold heads.

"This thing is a souvenir I picked up in Jamaica," he explained.

"Not a souvenir; demons with power," one man warned.

He laughed.

"I don't believe in mumbo-jumbo," he answered.

"Have you felt tired lately?" the man asked.

"I have, why?" he asked

"Those demons drain your life force," the man explained.

George dismissed the information and walked to Chelsea's Pub for a beer. He watched several people playing darts, and some of the players were good. There was no way for him to beat them, but it was a challenge. However, in the end, he reigned supreme. Later, he went to bed early because he felt exhausted.

The next morning, he felt like a truck had run him over, and when he looked in the mirror, he noted several gray hairs, which weren't there the day before.

While at work, Robert Downton, his supervisor, approached him.

"Are you feeling okay, George?" Robert asked.

"Been a bit under the weather," he answered.

"We have an important meeting in one hour," Robert said. "So, I hope you are up to the task, and for God's sake, remove that chain!"

He hated Robert because he mistreated people. He tried to take the chain off, but he received an electrical shock, and so, he buttoned up his collar. When he went to the meeting, he made Robert look unprepared.

"Why did you make me look like a fool in front of our clients?" Robert asked.

"Don't blame me, Robert. You didn't do your homework," he replied.

"You're right, I'm sorry. It's just that I'm stressed about my upcoming bonus," Robert explained.

"Robert, there are more things in life than money," he said.

"Let the broke man speak," Robert said with a laugh.

During lunch, he went to find the old Jamaican men, but they weren't at their usual spot. He then went inside Starbucks for coffee and a muffin, and then he spotted them outside.

"How do I get rid of this chain?" he asked.

"You must give it as a gift to someone living in excess," the man said.

"I know who deserves this more than me, but I must use its powers to convince him to take it off my hands," he said.

He returned to work to find Robert.

"Robert, if you want that bonus, meet me at Belmont racetrack this Saturday, and I'll show you how to secure it," he stated.

The next Saturday, they met at Belmont.

"I'm here, so show me!" Robert said.

"I will bet my savings on any three races you pick, and I will win all three," he said.

"You know that's highly improbable," Robert said.

"Do you want that bonus or not?" George asked.

Robert picked three long shots, and George won them, but in doing so, he lost several years of his life. He then understood why that Jamaican woman looked so old.

"How?" Robert asked.

"This is how," he pointed to his chain.

"That ugly thing?" Robert asked.

"That ugly thing just won me a lot of money," he said.

"Why would you give it up?" Robert asked.

"I am only lending it to you, so you'll get the bonus you truly deserve," he said.

The dollar signs flashed in Robert's eyes.

"Here you go, it's all yours," he said.

Robert got his bonus, but he refused to return the chain. George resigned and moved to California to sell real estate. Although he was only 25 years old, he looked fifty, and the women swooned all over him. Robert had made millions in his portfolio, but because of his rapid aging, it became too much and he jumped to his death. When he hit the sidewalk below, the three-headed chain shattered.

The End

Scratch and Sniff

As Jesse danced with one of the most beautiful women he had ever met, she displayed a lustful smile, and he knew what it meant. He took her to the Sleepers Inn Motel, where he had sex with various women. He paid his friend, Paul, the usual fifty to use a vacant room for a couple of hours. When they got inside the room, they undressed.

"I like my meat fresh," the woman said.

He thought that was a strange thing to say, but he still followed her into the shower. As he stood there, she scrubbed every inch of his toned body. He never had a woman wash him in such an erotic way before, and he was getting excited.

Afterward, she dried him off, and then herself.

When they exited the bathroom, she pushed him onto the bed, and he was surprised by her strength. She began licking him with her abnormally large tongue, which was getting him further excited. She had him turn over onto his stomach. When she finished licking, she scratched his back with one of her long sharp fingernails.

"What the fuck?" Jesse yelled.

She didn't say a word as she sniffed the blood and then licked it off his skin. As he tried to look back, he didn't have time to scream because the werewolf bit his head off and mutilated his body. Afterward, the creature turned back into a woman, and she went to wash the blood off her face. She got dressed, took Jesse's things, and drove away in his car.

Two hours later, Paul wondered about Jesse because he always brought the key back. When he walked to the room, he noticed that Jesse's car was gone.

"The room is probably a fucking mess," he grumbled.

When he looked inside, he saw Jesse's ripped apart body and screamed. The motel guests gathered near the room, and one of them was a psychiatrist. After he looked inside the room, he stood guard and told another guest to call the police.

Twenty minutes later, a sheriff's deputy arrived.

"What happened here?" the deputy asked.

"I wish the hell I knew," Dr. Burns said.

"What do you mean?" he asked.

"Have a look for yourself, and then you tell me!" Dr. Burns replied.

He took one look and closed the door.

"What the fuck happened in there?" he asked.

"From the looks of things, whoever is in there was killed by a large, powerful animal," Dr. Burns answered.

"What could do that to a body?" he asked.

"We won't know until we get DNA evidence," Dr. Burns replied.

"I'll call the medical examiner," he said.

A half-hour later, Dr. Philson arrived.

"Where's the body?" Dr. Philson asked.

"In there," the deputy pointed.

"Who found it?" Dr. Philson asked.

"Paul Larkin," he answered.

"I need to speak to him," Dr. Philson said.

"You can't because he's in shock, and I had to sedate him," Dr. Burns said.

"We need to find out what happened," Dr. Philson asked.

"Not until tomorrow," Dr. Burns replied.

"What kind of doctor are you?" Dr. Philson asked.

"A psychiatrist," Dr. Burns answered.

"Is he under your care?" Dr. Philson asked.

"Are you asking me to stay?" Dr. Burns asked.

"It would be best since we don't have a psychiatrist in town," Dr. Philson said.

"I would stay if my meals and room are comped for my services," Dr. Burns said.

"I can arrange that," Dr. Philson said. "Does anyone know the victim?"

"Mr. Larkin said something about 'Jesse,'" Dr. Burns replied.

"I hope to God that this isn't 'Little Jesse' in there!" Dr. Philson said.

As he looked for body parts, he found Jesse's head.

"It's him, alright!" Dr. Philson said.

"Fuck!" the deputy exclaimed.

"Who's the victim's father?" Dr. Burns asked.

"Jesse Williams, the most powerful man in the state," the deputy explained.

"I should talk to him before you two have heart attacks," Dr. Burns said.

"I'll drive you to his ranch," the deputy offered.

Before being allowed through the gate, armed guards searched them. Once they were deemed harmless, they were allowed to proceed.

"How far is the main house from here?" Dr. Burns asked.

"Another ten miles," the deputy said.

"How big is his ranch?" Dr. Burns asked.

"About five hundred square miles," he answered.

Dr. Burns let out a long whistle.

As they arrived at the main house, they were escorted inside by an armed guard.

"What's my son done this time?" Mr. Williams asked sternly.

"It's not what he did, but what happened to him," the deputy said nervously.

"I don't have all fucking night!" Mr. Williams said impatiently.

"We found him dead inside a motel room," Dr. Burns said.

"Who killed my son?" Mr. Williams asked angrily.

"It wasn't a who, but a what," Dr. Burns answered.

"What do you mean?" Mr. Williams asked angrily.

"His body was dismembered," Dr. Burns said.

"How is that possible?" Mr. Williams asked.

"We won't know until we get DNA evidence," the deputy answered.

"I want to see his body!" Mr. Williams demanded.

"I wouldn't recommend it, Mr. Williams," Dr. Burns suggested.

"He's my son, and I have the right to see him," Mr. Williams insisted.

"I'm sure that Dr. Philson has moved his body to the morgue," the deputy said.

"I want you two fucking assholes off my ranch!" Mr. Williams shouted.

The deputy and Dr. Burns drove back to town.

The next morning, Dr. Burns and the deputy met Dr. Philson at the morgue.

"How did Mr. Williams respond?" Dr. Burns asked.

"Not very well, as you can imagine," Dr. Philson replied. "He lost his wife to cancer three years ago, and Jesse was his only child."

"Did you find any DNA evidence on his body?" Dr. Burns asked.

"Besides the large bite marks, I found animal hair," Dr. Philson answered.

"What kind of animal hair?" the deputy asked.

"It looks like wolf hair," Dr. Philson said.

"Where did you send the evidence?" Dr. Burns asked.

"I sent it over to Dr. Shamus, the veterinarian," Dr. Philson replied. "He said he could identify the animal that killed Jesse by tomorrow."

"I hope the chief returns soon," the deputy said.

"He doesn't know about Jesse's death?" Dr. Philson asked.

"You know he doesn't have a phone in his cabin," the deputy said.

"It's not like him to be this late coming back from a fishing trip," Dr. Philson said.

"If he isn't back by tomorrow morning, I'll drive up to check on him," the deputy said.

"How far is his cabin from here?" Dr. Burns asked.

"About an hour drive," the deputy said.

"If it's okay, I'd like to tag along," Dr. Burns offered.

"Sure," the deputy replied.

After the deputy dropped Dr. Burns off at the motel, he returned to his office. When he walked in, he had a telephone message waiting. Jesse's car and wallet had been found in the next town over. He then began writing his crime report for the chief, which he finished at 5:00 pm. He locked the office and headed to the diner to meet Dr. Burns, and they both had steak for dinner.

"Any word from the chief?" Dr. Burns asked.

"Not a word," the deputy replied. "Did you ever watch werewolf movies?"

"Of course, why?" Dr. Burns asked.

"Do you think they could exist?" he asked.

"I don't believe in monsters if that's what you're asking," Dr. Burns responded.

"It's just strange how someone could be ripped apart in a motel room, and no one heard a thing," he said.

The deputy received a call from Dr. Shamus, asking him to stop by.

"I need to see Dr. Shamus; would you like to come along?" he asked.

"Okay," Dr. Burns replied.

They arrived at Dr. Shamus's animal practice, and as they walked to the front door, it was slightly ajar. The deputy called out to Dr. Shamus, but there was no reply. Suddenly, he appeared out of nowhere, making them jump.

"What was it that you wanted to tell me, Dr. Shamus?" the deputy asked.

"I examined the teeth marks and the hair, and it's not from any known species. So, tomorrow I'm going to the city to confer with a colleague," Dr. Shamus said.

"Thanks for the information, Dr. Shamus," he said.

As they drove away, they talked.

"Do you know the club where Jesse Williams met that woman?" Dr. Burns asked.

"Yes, it's called El Tigre," he said.

"I feel like having a drink," Dr. Burns asked.

"The club doesn't open until 9:00 pm, and it's only 8:20," he said.

"While we wait, we can observe the guests," Dr. Burns explained.

They parked outside the club to watch, but no one caught their eye until an extraordinarily beautiful woman walked into the club.

"Let's have that drink now," Dr. Burns suggested.

They walked into the bar, and both ordered rum and coke. As they watched the woman, she danced with both men and women, and then she looked directly at them with fiercely glowing eyes, making her message clear.

"What was that?" the deputy asked.

"She doesn't want us watching her," Dr. Burns replied.

"She gave me the creeps with those glowing eyes!" he exclaimed.

"I have never seen eyes like that before," Dr. Burns said.

The next morning, they drove to the chief's cabin. When the deputy and Dr. Burns, arrived, the stench of death permeated the air.

"You don't think...the chief's dead?" the deputy asked.

"At least three days," Dr. Burns replied.

Since they didn't have any Vicks VapoRub with them, they used lip balm to plug their noses. When they walked inside, they saw the chief. The deputy called the state troopers. After they arrived, Dr. Burns and the deputy drove back to town. Twenty minutes later, they spotted a rolled over SUV and stopped.

"That looks like Dr. Shamus's Range Rover," the deputy said.

They found Dr. Shamus's dismembered body and his briefcase, which was open.

"Whatever killed Dr. Shamus knew he had DNA evidence," the deputy said.

They heard rustling in the forest, and they couldn't believe what they saw. A monstrous wolf with two giant glowing eyes looking at them, and then it left.

"I have never seen a wolf that huge," Dr. Burns observed.

"Maybe we should rethink the werewolf theory," he suggested.

"I agree," Dr. Burns said. "Where were Dr. Shamus and the chief from?"

"They went to high school together," he replied.

"And Mr. Williams?" Dr. Burns asked.

"What are you getting at?" he inquired.

"I don't think these murders were random," Dr. Burns responded. "Something from their past got them killed."

"How about little Jesse?" he asked.

"Maybe something his father did," Dr. Burns said. "When we went to tell him about his son, I think we led her right to him, and now she's on her way there to kill him."

"Who is this? 'She' you're referring?" he asked.

"We met her at the club last night," Dr. Burns said.

"You think she's a werewolf?" he asked.

"I recognized something in that wolf's eyes, and it was her," Dr. Burns said.

When they arrived at the front gate, the guards were missing.

"We may be too late," Dr. Burns surmised.

They sped toward the main ranch house, and after they arrived, they crept to the front door. When they went inside, they heard loud growling. When they walked into the den, the monstrous werewolf was close to Mr. Williams.

"Don't kill him!" Dr. Burns said.

The werewolf suddenly turned back into the woman.

"Why shouldn't I?" she asked.

"You're supposed to be dead!" Mr. Williams exclaimed.

"After you and your friends raped me, beat me close to death, and put me in that shallow grave, I was saved by a race of polymorph aliens. In doing so, they turned me into a monster," she explained. "I should thank you two for leading me right to this evil bastard. He and his friends have been raping and killing women since high school, and because he's rich, he'll get off, but I know where they buried six of their victims," she said.

"Where?" the deputy asked.

"In the last two horse stalls beneath the cement floor because I can smell them," she replied.

"Well, Mr. Williams, I believe you'll be getting the death penalty," Dr. Burns said.

"Not on my watch," Mr. Williams answered.

He shot the woman and then himself.

"Thank you," she said on her dying breath.

Two hours later, the state troopers arrived. They found six female bodies buried at the location where the woman said they were.

"So, who did all of the killings?" Trooper Smith asked.

"Mr. Williams, Chief Andrews, and Dr. Shamus were raping and killing young women since high school. I believe that his son learned the truth, and Mr. Williams killed him to keep him quiet, but then Mr. Williams decided to tie up loose ends. I believe the dead woman over there, confronted him, and when we walked into the house, we heard two gunshots. He must have shot her and then killed himself," the deputy said.

"There were rumors about a giant wolf roaming in these parts," Trooper Smith told them.

"Like I told the deputy, there are no such things as monsters," Dr. Burns said.

The End

The Pearl of Andromeda

CATHERINE WAS THE only child of Chance Beckman, a wealthy arms manufacturer, and her mother, Sarah Foster-Beckman, a clothing designer. When Catherine turned six, her parents chose to have her homeschooled rather than send her to public school. What surprised the tutors the most about Catherine was her uniquely keen intellect, realizing she was heading for greatness, and yet she had difficulty handing-in her assignments on time, if at all.

At the age of eight, Catherine had her parents wrapped around her little finger, and they got her everything she wanted because they felt guilty for not spending time with her.

When Catherine argued with her parents or a household staff member, she would find a way back into their hearts, but they never realized that she wanted affection. In time, she became aloof.

After a while, the staff walked around her on egg-shells because her horrid behavior was wearing thin.

At the age of twelve, Cat, as she called herself, was caught shoplifting, but being a clever girl, she got off with a warning. She wasn't a bad girl at heart, but she was slowly losing her identity by keeping everything bottled up inside.

At the age of fourteen, Cat got admitted to a private academy for exceptionally gifted students. As a limousine drove her away, the staff happily waved goodbye.

In her junior year at the academy, someone introduced her to ecstasy at a college frat party, and she liked the way it made her feel. From there, she moved on to excessive drinking and cocaine. As her behavior became erratic, they dismissed her from the academy.

Cat's parents came to realize just how much their absenteeism impacted her life when a judge issued a court order forcing them to send their daughter to a drug and alcohol rehabilitation center. Upon her return, they brought in a family therapist.

Six months later, her parents died when their small plane crashed in the mountains.

At the reading of the Beckman Will, Cat inherited the entire estate, and each household staff member received a substantial payment for each year of faithful service. Upon receiving their checks after the reading, the household staff resigned, leaving Cat alone.

Grieving the loss of her parents and loneliness began to take its toll, and she started drinking again, but that wasn't enough to hide her pain. Since she no longer had a trusted drug source, she went onto the Dark Web to find a local supplier.

After being up on a three-day alcohol and Cocaine bender, she remembered the pills the dealer gave her when she needed sleep, but what she didn't know was they contained Fentanyl. The next day that same dealer was arrested for two Fentanyl related deaths. She was about to take the pills when a bright light pierced her eyes. As the light dimmed, a woman of regal distinction appeared. As Cat looked at the woman, she resembled an elf, but her skin sparkled like glitter, her eyes glowed, and her hair was raven black hiding bluish pointed ears.

"Who are you?" Cat asked curiously.

"I am Princess Almea, a representative of the Interplanetary Council of Elders. As I look upon you, their judgment comes into question because you are not worthy to receive their gift because you are about to end your life with poison," she said.

"Wait...what?" Cat asked, dropping the pills.

"Calm your mind, Catherine of Earth," she said with a wave of her hand.

Suddenly Cat felt a calmness she had never experienced.

"What did you do to me?" Cat asked.

"Just a simple demonstration of the power you are to receive," she said.

"Can you show me more?" Cat asked.

The Princess suddenly held a ball of light in her hands.

"What is that?" Cat asked.

"It's called The Pearl of Andromeda, the gift the council sent to you. You may touch it if you like," she said.

Cat felt an incredible power, and she wanted more because it made her feel alive, but Princess Almea backed away.

"Catherine of Earth, I am giving you one Earth year to ready yourself, or the Interplanetary Council of Elders must select another to represent them," she said.

"How can I do as you ask if I haven't a clue as to what I am supposed to do?" Cat asked.

"Since the council chose you, I will provide you a mentor," she said.

"Mentor?" Cat asked.

Suddenly, a strange glowing disk hung around her neck.

"What's this?" Cat asked.

"Your mentor," she said.

"This piece of old junk?" Cat asked.

"Catherine of Earth, I am not a piece of junk," a female voice said. Cat nearly fainted.

"Catherine of Earth, meet Alliandra, and if it were me, I would apologize," she said.

"I... I'm very sorry, Alliandra, I didn't know," Cat said.

"Apology accepted, Catherine of Earth, and it's nice to meet my student," Alliandra said.

"Before I take my leave of you, Catherine of Earth, I give you fair warning. Alliandra will be reporting your progress directly to me," she said.

Princess Almea suddenly vanished.

"What am I supposed to do now, Alliandra?" Cat asked.

"We begin your lessons from self-awareness to enlightenment," Alliandra said.

"More school work!" Cat said with dismay.

"I understand your reluctance, but the true strength of a flower lies in its ability to grow and later spread its seed," Alliandra said.

"What does that supposed to mean?" Cat asked.

"It implies that you have much to learn, Catherine of Earth," Alliandra said. "Therefore, if you do not apply yourself, Princess Almea will return to introduce me to another student."

"I'm sorry, Alliandra, but my mind is a bit fuzzy after all the drinking and drugs I've been using," Cat said.

"Before we begin, I must repair the damage caused to your brain," Alliandra said.

"How can you fix me if you're Artificial Intelligence?" Cat asked.

"I am not an artificial life form, Catherine of Earth," Alliandra stated. "I am a living being with consciousness such as yourself, but lacking a body."

"Wait…what?" Cat asked.

"My body sustained massive injuries in a war fought long ago, and I have been residing inside a Crystalline Star Matrix ever since," Alliandra said.

"So, you're like a genie in a bottle?" Cat asked.

"An interesting perspective, but yes," Alliandra said.

"Where do you come from?" Cat asked.

"Both the princess and I are from Abanthia, one of the Unified Planets of the Andromeda Galaxy," Alliandra said.

"Did you say, Andromeda?" Cat asked.

"I did, Catherine of Earth," Alliandra said.

"It would take us two million years to travel from here to there, so how can you travel in such a short time?" Cat asked.

"We have discovered a way to interconnect stable wormholes, which allows us to travel great distances much quicker," Alliandra said.

"I see, but what are you doing on Earth?" Cat asked.

"We have been observing distant planets seeking a humanoid species similar to us. Although we prefer a peaceful coexistence with other alien species, we come in contact, there are those that war is a way of life, and they use assassins," Alliandra said.

"Why did the council choose me?" Cat asked.

"You were chosen before birth, Catherine of Earth. While you were living inside your mother's womb, we gave you your intelligence. When you are ready, the council will allow you to speak on their behalf to offer Earth their protection," Alliandra said.

"What about the assassins?" Cat asked.

"There is no need to worry, Catherine of Earth, because our enemies have no idea what we've been planning, and once you receive your gift, you will have powers to protect you from harm," Alliandra said.

"Does that mean my powers could be a weapon?" Cat asked.

"They chose you to be an envoy for peace, but your powers could be a weapon to keep warmongering alien species from attacking protected planets," Alliandra said.

"I'm not sure about any of this!" Cat said.

"Are you ready to be healed?" Alliandra asked.

"I guess," Cat said.

A blue light encompassed her entire body, and moments later, she felt different.

"What did you do to me?" Cat asked.

"I healed the damaged parts of your brain, but I cannot heal your grief because that is something you must do on your own," Alliandra said.

Suddenly, Cat's life flashed before her eyes, and she fell onto the bed, crying.

The next day, Alliandra woke her wishing her a good morning.

"Are you ready to begin your lessons?" Alliandra asked.

"Let's begin tomorrow because there are a few things I need to do first," Cat said.

She flushed the remaining drugs down the toilet, poured every bottle of alcohol down the kitchen sink, and then she bagged up her old clothing to donate. She then made several calls to hire a house cleaning service, a personal chef to do her shopping and cooking, a personal assistant to help with her daily affairs and scheduling, and a landscaper. Afterward, she showered and went shopping. Instead of buying her typical style of clothing, she bought the clothes of a young businesswoman. What emerged was Ms. Catherine Eloise Beckman.

"Alliandra, you may call me Cat, and I will call you, Ali," she said.

"As you wish," Ali said.

"Besides my lessons, I want to use my resources to help others," Cat said.

"First, we must focus on you," Ali said.

"Me? Why?" she asked.

"To be able to help others effectively, you must be your highest self," Ali said.

Eleven months later, Cat's old version of herself had vanished completely, and she and Ali became best friends.

"Where do we go from here, Ali?" Cat asked. "Don't answer, I hear Brenda coming."

"Who were you talking to, Ms. Beckman?" Brenda asked.

"Just an old friend on the phone, so what's on the agenda for today?" Catherine asked.

"Your meeting with Mayor Thomas is at 1:00 pm about the city's homeless population problem," Brenda said. "Also, Father Jake's Food Bank just called thanking you for your wonderful donation because they were able to expand their services to another location."

"That's good to hear," Catherine said. "Have we heard from the City Council about my Clean City Initiative?"

"Nothing yet, Ma'am," Brenda said.

"I will also be discussing that with Mayor Thomas," Catherine said.

"Is there anything else, Ma'am?" Brenda asked.

"You can start calling me, Cat," she said.

"Are you sure, Ma'am?" Brenda asked.

"I am sure, Brenda," she said. "Would you like to go to lunch, and you can choose where."

"How does the Olive Garden sound?" Brenda asked.

"Your choice, my treat," Cat said.

They had a great conversation during lunch. Catherine learned that Brenda, like herself, had no living relatives. After lunch, Catherine went to her appointment using her limousine service while Brenda drove back to the mansion.

During her meeting with the mayor, Catherine offered to renovate several closed motels for the homeless in the city. She told the mayor that each room would have a small bathroom with a shower, a single bed, and a heavy metal entry door with a deadbolt. The mayor was delighted by her proposal. As she walked out of his office, an assassin killed Brenda, but she wasn't the target.

Suddenly, Catherine's phone rang with an unfamiliar ringtone, and she answered it.

"Brenda is dead, so we must hurry back to the mansion," Ali said.

"Oh, my God!" Cat cried out.

"I contacted Princess Almea, and she should be waiting for us," Ali said.

As Cat ran into her office, she cried when she saw Brenda's lifeless body lying on the floor, and then she spotted Princess Almea in the corner.

"My assassin will pay dearly for his mistake!" she blurted out.

"Why do you want me dead?" Cat asked.

"Because I deserve to be the Pearl of Andromeda, not you!" she snarled.

"Then take it, it's yours," Cat said.

"Catherine of Earth, the gift can only be accepted by you, but if I kill you and destroy Alliandra, I can convince the council to let me be the Pearl of Andromeda," she said.

Ali was transmitting the conversation to the council.

"The only reason you want it is to have the power over life and death," Cat said.

"Who better to wield such power," she said.

"You should read more fairytales to see what happens to evil bitches like you?" Cat said.

"I am royalty, and you should address me as such," she said.

"You will pay dearly for killing Brenda, your highness," Cat said.

Suddenly, the princess had a weapon aimed at Cat.

"Say goodbye, Catherine of Earth," she said.

Ali fired a red beam at the princess, and she suddenly vanished.

"What happened to her?" Cat asked.

"The council told me to dispatch her," Ali said.

"Does that mean she's dead?" Cat asked.

"No, her consciousness will live on inside a Crystalline Matrix-like me," Ali explained.

"How are we going to explain Brenda's death to the police?" Cat asked.

"What happens next is up to you," Ali said.

"What do you mean?" Cat asked.

"Since humans are less complex lifeforms, I can transfer my consciousness into Brenda's body, but the decision to do so is yours," Ali said.

"Well, she doesn't have any living relatives, so I don't see a problem," Cat said.

Ali transferred her consciousness into Brenda, but she had difficulty with her balance because it's been two thousand years since she's occupied a living body.

"I think this will take a few minutes," Ali said.

Ali eventually hugged Cat tightly and told her that she loved her.

"I love you too," Cat responded, kissing her on the lips.

"Are you ready?" Ali asked.

"For what?" Cat asked.

Ali was holding the Pearl of Andromeda.

"It's time, and we don't have a moment to waste," Ali said.

"Can its power be shared?" Cat asked.

"I don't know," Ali said.

"How does it work?" Cat asked.

"Once I give the command, it becomes a part of you," Ali said.

"Let's stand close with it between us," Cat suggested.

They grasped onto each other's forearms with the Pearl of Andromeda floating between them. As Ali gave the command, they both absorbed its power. Afterward, two elders appeared.

"Catherine of Earth and Alliandra of Andromeda, you have fulfilled your destiny. We, the ones who created The Pearl of Andromeda, designed it to be shared by two in body, mind, and spirit," an elder said.

"Does that mean that the council is ready to contact Earth?" Cat asked.

"It does, Catherine of Earth," the elder said. "But first, Alliandra must instruct you on the use of your new powers."

"When should I approach Earth's leaders?" Cat asked.

"At the end of three months, Catherine of Earth, because your planet is on the precipice of extinction," the elder said.

"How much time does Earth have left?" Cat asked.

"Five years, possibly less," the elder said.

"Can it be stopped?" she asked.

"Only if Earth becomes a member of the Interplanetary Council," the elder said.

"So, your protection is our only recourse for survival?" Cat asked.

"It is," the elder said.

The elders vanished.

Two months later, Cat understood her new powers with the help of Ali, and then they were joined together during an interplanetary wedding ceremony.

In the following month, Cat and Ali entered a closed session of the United Nations. Everyone was in a tizzy over their unexpected arrival as they walked to the podium with a glowing aura. Cat waved her hand at the speaker, and he sat in a chair.

"Ladies and Gentlemen of the United Nations Assembly and the world, I am here to introduce you to Catherine, the Pearl of Andromeda," Ali said.

Cat slowly walks to the podium.

"People of Earth, I am Catherine, who serves the Interplanetary Council as their Envoy of peace. The question, whether life exists beyond the stars, has been answered," she stated.

Everyone on Earth was shocked by this unexpected revelation.

"I must now beg your forgiveness because I must speak bluntly. The Interplanetary Council of Elders has watched our Earth for thousands of years, and it's time for us to become a member, but changes are necessary. Our lands, oceans, and skies are becoming unsustainable, and within five years, maybe less, life on Earth will cease to exist. I am not here to frighten you, but to present you with the facts. Our only option to survive as a species is to become a member of the council. So, what happens when we become a council member? Our lands will be pristine again when our refuse is taken to gigantic plants to convert matter into energy for powering vast alien civilizations. Our precious water and skies will also be clean again. In other words, Earth will become new, but at what cost?" she said.

- We will provide sand from our deserts to save the last remaining Island in Oceania.
- We will provide our refuse to power alien cities.
- We will provide our precious metals to power alien spacecraft. In return, they will give us a clean and safe power source, but once it's in place, all coal mining, nuclear power plants, and oil production operations will cease.

The members of the United Nations started yelling at her, and she raised her hand to silence them.

"If we continue down our current path, extinction is assured. If that be your wish, so be it, but if you choose life, then you must accept the council's offer. I have before me a list of requirements that we must complete, or face extinction.

- All nuclear weapons must be deactivated.
- Our government's corruption will end.

- Our educational system will undergo a significant shift.
- Known diseases, including mental illness, will cease to exist.
- Homelessness and hunger will cease to exist.
- And, our militaries will become a unified peacekeeping force.

"The decision to save Earth is yours!" Catherine said.

The End

The Magical Mystical Detective Winterstorm

POLICE OFFICERS, PENELOPE Wynterbourne and Wayne Hendricks, were dispatched to a Jewelry store heist in progress. When they drove into the parking lot, the employees were standing up against the front window, blocking their view of the inside. After Officer Wynterbourne radioed in, dispatch told her to standby until other units arrived, and then a woman screamed.

"Did you hear that Wayne?" Penelope asked.

"I did, but dispatch told us to wait," he said.

The woman screamed again.

"Don't do it, Penelope," he said.

"Fuck you, Wayne," she yelled.

As she approached the backdoor of the jewelry store, it suddenly flew open, and she was shot twice with a 12-gauge pump shotgun. When she landed on the pavement, she broke her spine in two places, her pelvis, and right hip. The man who shot her laughed as he went back inside, and then a tiny being sent her thoughts to her as she lay dying on the cold hard payment.

"Who are you, and why are you in my head?" she asked.

"Like you, waiting for death," the voice replied.

"I'm not afraid to die," she said.

"I knew I picked the right woman," the voice said.

"What does that mean?" she asked.

"If we could live as one being, would you do it to survive?" the voice asked.

"How much time do I have to think about it?" she asked.

"You don't have much time because your organs are failing," the voice said.

"I may regret it later, but okay!" she answered.

A few moments later, she was miraculously healed and picked herself off the ground. She then went inside the jewelry store to find the man who shot her. As she crept inside, she saw him watching two of his men trying to rape a female employee. He caught a glimpse of Officer Wynterbourne, and he attempted to shoot her a second time, but this time, she shot first. He and his shotgun hit the floor, breaking his right arm. She then told the other two men to get away from the woman and to lie face down on the floor.

The other units arrived five minutes later, finding three suspects on the floor. They were arrested and escorted out. A few minutes later, Officer Hendricks appeared.

"I thought you were dead," he said.

"Who told you that?" she asked.

"The suspect you shot said he shot you with his shotgun," he replied.

"That could have happened since you blindly followed orders!" she barked.

"Then why is there blood on your uniform, and it's shredded like cheese?" he asked. "Anyway, the chief wants to see you right away."

Thirty minutes later, she was face-to-face with Chief Dickens.

"This is the third time you disobeyed my direct orders?" he yelled.

"I had to act alone because Officer Hendricks stayed in the cruiser while two men were trying to rape a woman!" she yelled back.

"From what he told me, you're lucky to be alive!" he yelled.

"We're supposed to be protecting our citizens, but you and Officer Hendricks are incapable of doing just that!" she screamed back.

"I want your gun and badge on my desk, NOW!" he yelled.

She slammed them down on his desk.

"You can stick both of them up your ass," she yelled.

She gathered her things and left the building.

"You didn't need that job," the voice said.

"You are real!" she replied.

"Yes," the voice said.

"I thought I'd imagined you," she said. "Can anyone else hear you?"

"Only you," the voice said.

"Do you have a name?" she asked.

"Sa'Rhi," the voice said. "And yours?"

"Penelope," she offered. "May I ask what you are?"

"I'll explain over chocolate ice cream," Sa'Rhi said.

"How can you eat ice cream?" she asked.

"I can't, but as a part of you, I can taste whatever you eat or drink, and I choose chocolate ice cream," Sa'Rhi said.

She drove to Baskin-Robbins, ordered two scoops of chocolate ice cream in a cup, and then returned to her car.

"I'm glad you suggested chocolate ice cream. It's so relaxing," Penelope said.

"It's heavenly," Sa'Rhi said. "But, I promised you an explanation."

"Okay, I'm listening," she said.

"I'm from the interdimensional realm of Ba'Kar, the watchers of Earth's Multiverse of Twelve. I was sent to this time to influence President Johnson, whom I discovered wasn't born yet, and when I tried to return home through the portal, it was closed," Sa'Rhi said.

"Have you considered the idea that someone wanted you out of the way," she said.

"It had to be my brother because I'm next to rule where my father reigns, but since we're now in a symbiotic relationship, I can never return home," Sa'Rhi said sadly.

"Does that mean we're together until I die?" she asked.

"It's the other way around," Sa'Rhi said.

"How long does your kind live?" she asked.

"A thousand or more Earth years," Sa'Rhi responded.

"How old are you now?" she asked.

"I just turned three hundred," Sa'Rhi stated.

"Are you telling me that I'll be an old bag of bones before I die?" she retorted.

"You've already stopped aging," Sa'Rhi said.

"What?" she retorted. "And you didn't bother telling me this before I accepted your offer!"

"If I did, we wouldn't be enjoying this delicious chocolate ice cream?" Sa'Rhi said.

"I'm sorry," she said. "I should be thankful that you saved my life."

"And you saved mine," Sa'Rhi said.

"How did I save your life?" she asked.

"Earth's gravity isn't compatible with our bodies, so, if we don't return through the portal by the eighth-day, we die," Sa'Rhi said.

"Is joining with humans something your kind does?" she asked.

"You're the first human that a symbiotic relationship has ever been tried," Sa'Rhi said.

"So, we're operating in new territory?" she asked.

"Yes, and I have no idea how it will affect us," Sa'Rhi said.

"I guess at the time; we were both in a hurt locker," she said.

"What's a hurt locker?" Sa'Rhi asked.

"It means a bad situation, but I think it's time for some tequila shots!" she said.

"What are those?" Sa'Rhi asked.

"You'll soon find out," she answered.

When she walked into her favorite bar, she saw Wayne sitting alone on a barstool drinking a draft beer. She walked up behind him and yelled, "GO FUCK YOURSELF, WAYNE." He spilled the beer all over himself and left the bar, embarrassed.

The very next morning, her alarm clock went off its usual time, and she tossed it across the room. When she finally awoke, it was early afternoon.

"What happened last night because my right-hand is sore?" she asked.

"Two men tried to rob you outside the bar," Sa'Rhi said.

"What happened to them?" she asked.

"You put them in a hurt locker," Sa'Rhi said.

Penelope fell back on the bed, laughing.

"I guess it's time to shower because I smell like a brewery," she said.

As she passed the mirror, she took two steps back for a double-take. Her hair was now raven black, her skin, smooth alabaster, her eyes, cobalt blue, and her ears pointed.

"Why the fuck do I look like an elf from the Hobbit movies?" she asked angrily.

As she looked at herself more closely, she noticed other changes. The day before, her cheeks had acne scars, her nose was bulbous, her lips were fuller than most, and now she was a strikingly beautiful woman. Her curiosity was piqued, and she removed her pajamas and undergarments. As she examined her body, her once droopy muffin-top mid-drift was perfectly flat with visible abs, her breasts were slightly smaller yet nicely rounded, and her arms and legs were perfectly toned and muscular. She was ecstatic by her surprising transformation.

After showering, she went shopping for an entirely new wardrobe and wore a cap to cover her pointed ears. As she went from store to store, men couldn't help but stare at her.

When she returned home, she went online to search for employment opportunities. She had no idea what she wanted to do because she had imagined herself retiring as a police officer. She then came across two private investigation agencies looking for investigators, and she applied.

Afterward, she went to the Department of Motor Vehicles for a new driver's license. A female employee was skeptical by her unique appearance, but Penelope told her that she recently had facial reconstructive and ear surgery, and dyed her hair black.

The very next day, she arrived for her first interview, but when she removed her cap, they didn't like her pointed ears and sent her away.

The next morning, she arrived for her second interview without the cap. After the lead detectives interviewed her, they agreed that she would be the perfect fit for undercover work because of her unique appearance. They offered her the job.

After two years with Carson Investigations, she left to open an investigative agency for herself, and she began the process of changing her name to Winterstorm because of her elf-like appearance and her latent magical abilities. When she looked for a place to open her business, she found a small building with an attached apartment.

A few weeks later, Winterstorm and Sa'Rhi were bored because they had only one investigation to their name after opening for business, and their cash reserves were running low. As they enjoyed a pint of chocolate ice cream, Winterstorm's phone rang.

"How did you get my private number, Mayor Wilson?" she asked.

"Carson Investigations gave it to me because we need help on a possible homicide case that has the medical examiner and the police baffled," he said.

"What's the case regarding?" she asked.

"The sudden death of Kevin Swanson," he said.

"Can the city afford my fee of two thousand dollars a day?" she asked.

"Are you joking, he said.

"No, so I guess this is where we part company," she responded.

"For heaven's sake Detective Winterstorm," he yelled.

"Was that a yes?" she asked.

"Yes," he said reluctantly.

"Okay, but I want to examine the body for myself," she said.

"I'll let the medical examiner know," he said.

"Thank you, Mayor Wilson," she said.

The mayor hung up.

"So, why do we need to examine his body, Sa'Rhi?" she asked.

"Because you'll be asking him questions," Sa'Rhi responded. "But, our window of opportunity is expiring soon."

"There's a time limit for talking to dead people?" she asked.

"The first three days after death," Sa'Rhi replied.

She drove to the medical examiner's office and told him that she wanted to be left alone as she examined the body, and he decided to have lunch.

"How do we proceed, Sa'Rhi?" she asked.

"Place your first and second fingers between his temples. Now, generate electrical impulses between the fingers with your mind, and then ask your questions."

"How were you killed Mr. Swanson?" she asked.

He said, "My scotch was drugged, and then poison injected into my brain."

And then nothing.

"That's all we'll get because his Astral Body faded away," Sa'Rhi said.

As she finished her examination, the medical examiner returned, and she asked him some questions.

"Did you find any puncture marks on his body?"

"I looked in the usual places, but I didn't find any," he said.

"Did you check his eyes?" she asked.

"No, I didn't think to look there," he said.

"If you look closely, there's a puncture mark in the conjunctiva of his left eye where someone injected poison," she said. "Since his body doesn't smell yet, I believe arsenic was the poison his murderer used to kill him, so check his urine for residual evidence. Also, you need to run a tox screen to see what drug they used to render him unconscious."

"I will do those tests immediately," he assured her.

Afterward, she drove to the police department. When she walked inside, she went to see Chief Myers, who replaced Chief Dickens after being terminated for gross incompetence.

"I need to see the case file for Mr. Swanson's murder," she asked.

"But the medical examiner…," she stopped him by holding her hand up.

"He missed crucial evidence during his examination, and he's running other tests at my request," she explained. "Also, if you wouldn't mind, I would like to review the file in private."

Officer Connors brought her the file, and then he and the chief waited by his desk.

"Who's that Chief?" he asked.

"The detective, Mayor Wilson hired," the chief said.

After she finished reviewing the file, she signaled Chief Myers to return to his office.

"I want you to bring Jason Markham and Mrs. Swanson in for questioning," she said.

He sent two police units to pick them up.

"Okay, they've arrived," he said.

"While we were waiting, the medical examiner called me to confirm my suspicions, but the evidence is circumstantial," she said.

"So, if we don't get a confession, they'll get away with murder?" he asked.

"Precisely, and that's why I want to interview Mrs. Swanson," she said.

As she walked into the room, Mrs. Swanson was smoking a cigarette.

"Who or what are you?" Mrs. Swanson asked curiously.

"I'm Detective Winterstorm, and I am here to have a chat with you like the one I had with Mr. Markham," she lied.

"What did he have to say?" Mrs. Swanson asked.

"Not much, except that you two were having an affair," she answered.

"I really wouldn't call it an affair, but we did have an occasional roll in the hay," Mrs. Swanson said.

As she continued the interview, her body began emitting a strange substance that affected Mrs. Swanson most peculiarly.

"You smell delicious," Mrs. Swanson said.

She caught Detective Winterstorm off guard, and she used it to her advantage.

"Does that mean you want me," she asked.

"More than anyone," Mrs. Swanson said.

"Okay, then tell me why you killed your husband," she said.

"I drugged the bastard's scotch because he was planning to divorce me for another woman, and take everything I earned away from me, so after he passed out, I let Jason Markham into the house to finish the job," Mrs. Swanson said.

"Did you get that, Officer Jennings?" she asked.

"Every word," he replied.

"I must go now, Mrs. Swanson," she said.

"Please stay; I need you," Mrs. Swanson begged.

After leaving the room, she knocked on the other door.

"What is it, Detective Winterstorm?" Chief Myers asked.

"We have Mrs. Swanson's confession, and she told me that Mr. Markham killed her husband," she said.

"Why that fucking bitch! She's the one who planned it," Mr. Markham said.

"Would you put that in writing?" the chief asked.

"Since I don't have anything to lose, why not?" he said.

As he wrote out his confession, the chief and she returned to his office.

"Thanks to you, Detective Winterstorm, we solved Mr. Swanson's murder," he said.

"The mayor hired me to do a job, and I did it!" she said.

After she walked out of the police department, she and Sa'Rhi talked.

"While I interviewed Mrs. Swanson, something odd happened," she said.

"You mean when she had a sudden desire for you, and then told you her darkest secret?" Sa'Rhi asked. "Your body released an aphrodisiac truth hormone."

"Is that something your kind does?" she asked.

"No, that's a new development," Sa'Rhi said.

"Then, I think we earned some tequila shots for a job well-done," she suggested.

"With salt and lime?" Sa'Rhi asked.

"Anyway, you like!" she said.

Two weeks later, they were practicing Winterstorm's developing abilities.

"Okay, now concentrate on the glass and wave your hand," Sa'Rhi said.

"It's not working!" she replied.

"Please, try again," Sa'Rhi said.

She concentrated harder on the glass, waved her hand, and it moved.

"You did it!" Sa'Rhi exclaimed.

"Yes, but now my head is pounding," she said.

"It's all that tequila you drank last night," Sa'Rhi commented.

"I know, and I want to crawl back into bed," she said.

Suddenly, their front office door opened, and a woman walked in crying.

"He's not my husband, he's not my husband," she said over and over again.

Winterstorm sat her down and had her breathe into a bag. After a few minutes, she was calm enough to speak.

"Please, tell me from the beginning," she told her.

"The man who says he's my husband isn't," the woman said.

"When did you notice the difference?" she asked.

"After he returned from his last business trip," the woman answered.

"Why do you think that he isn't your husband?" she asked.

"We've been married for twenty years, and I quickly noted the differences," the woman replied.

"What would you like me to do?" she asked.

"I want to hire you to look into it for me?" the woman asked.

"Okay, but I need your name," she asked.

"Victoria Payson," the woman replied.

"May I call you Victoria?" she asked.

"Please, do," the woman replied.

"My fee is $2,000 a day plus expenses, is that alright with you?" she stated.

"Yes," Victoria said.

"Do you feel safe at home?" she asked.

"Not with that stranger," Victoria answered.

"Would you call him to say that you're going to visit an old friend named Penelope Wynterbourne," she suggested.

"Who is that?" Victoria asked.

"Someone I once knew," she said.

"And the reason?" Victoria asked.

"To verify if he's an imposter, or not," she said. "Does your husband know all of your friends?"

"He does," Victoria said.

"Then, if he says okay, we know he's an imposter," she said.

After Victoria made the call, she burst into tears.

"Do you have a place to stay for a few days?" she asked.

"We have a house in the Hamptons," Victoria said.

"That won't work because you need to be out of pocket," she replied.

"What does that mean?" Victoria asked.

"Not going to the usual haunts, contacting friends, or using your credit cards," she explained. "Do you have any cash reserves?"

"I have some money stashed away inside a safe deposit box under an alias at Chase Bank," Victoria said.

"What's your alias?" she asked.

"Barbara Williams," Victoria said.

"I will accompany you to the bank to make sure it's safe," she offered.

They drove to the bank and parked across the street.

"Why are we waiting?" Victoria asked.

"To see who goes in and who comes out," she said.

They watched for a few minutes when Winterstorm sees a man pacing back and forth outside the bank.

"Do you know that man over there?" she pointed.

"No, I never saw him before," Victoria answered.

"I believe someone is watching you," she said.

"By whom?" Victoria asked.

"That's what I'm about to find out," she replied.

"How?" Victoria asked.

"I will become your alias, Barbara Williams," she said.

"But, you don't look anything like me," Victoria said.

"Trust me," she said. "I have several tricks up my sleeve, so give me your license and safe deposit box key."

Winterstorm walked across the street into the bank. She waved her hand in front of the bank manager to create an illusion, so he sees her as Barbara Williams. She pretended to sign the signature card, and then he took her to the safe deposit box. After he inserted his key, and she hers, he took the safe deposit box to a private room, and then he left. She opened the box and put the money into her pocket. After walking outside, she walked up to the man pacing in front of the bank.

"Are you looking for me?" she asked.

"Why would I be looking for you?" the man asked.

"Because I just emptied Barbara Williams's safe deposit box," she replied.

Suddenly, she emitted that powerful pheromone.

"Why do you smell so delicious?" the man asked.

"Why are you after Barbara Williams?" she asked.

"Because she's not Barbara Williams, but Victoria Payson," he explained.

"How do you know her?" she asked.

"Her husband hired my agency yesterday to watch her," he replied.

"Are you a detective?" she asked.

"Yes, with Pinkerton in Phoenix," he answered.

"You will forget that we ever met," she said.

She walked across the street to her car.

"Who was he?" Victoria asked.

"A Pinkerton detective, your imposter husband hired," she asked.

"If he knows you have the money, why didn't he do anything?" Victoria asked.

"He believes that nothing happened," she replied.

"How?" Victoria asked.

"As I said, I have a few tricks up my sleeve," she said. "Before I forget, here's your moncy."

Victoria suddenly kissed her long and hard on the lips, but Winterstorm didn't fight it.

"Thanks," she said.

The pheromones finally wore off on the drive to the agency.

"Sorry I kissed you like that," Victoria said, embarrassed.

"You were just happy that I got your money," she answered.

She parked the car outside her agency, and then they went inside.

"Where do I go from here?" Victoria asked.

"Where did your husband go on his business trip?"

"Moscow," Victoria said.

"How often does he go there for business?" she asked.

"About once every two months," Victoria said.

"They must have made the body-double switch before he got on the plane," she said.

"Who are they?" Victoria asked.

"That's what I intend to find out," she responded. "I'll be on the first flight to Moscow to retrieve your husband."

She waved her hand across Victoria's face, putting her into a hypnotic state.

"I hope you enjoy your trip to Australia," she said.

"How can I ever thank you, Detective Winterstorm?" Victoria asked.

"No need to thank me. Just enjoy your vacation," Winterstorm said.

Victoria was taken to Winterstorm's apartment to enjoy her mind-cation.

"What about water, food, and bathing?" Sa'Rhi asked.

"She'll have the capacity to care for herself," she answered.

"Is that how a human kiss feels? Sa'Rhi asked.

"Yes, did you enjoy it?" she asked.

"It was oddly pleasurable, and it made me tingle," Sa'Rhi said.

"By the way, do we speak Russian?"

"Da," Sa'Rhi replied.

Ten hours later, Winterstorm was on her way to Moscow. The next day, as she passed through customs, the man checking her passport wanted to see if she had pointed ears. He made her remove her hat, and then he smiled.

"Welcome to Russia, Ms. Winterstorm," he said.

She took a taxi to the Renaissance Moscow Monarch Centre Hotel, where Mr. Payson stayed during his last trip. She checked in and retired to her suite, where she called room service for a bottle of tequila, limes, and salt. After tipping the concierge, she told him that she had a scheduled meeting with Mr. Payson, but he wasn't answering his phone. He said that Mr. Payson became ill and was rushed to the hospital a few days ago.

The concierge left.

"That confirms Mr. Payson's kidnapping," she said. "So, we're either dealing with the FSB or the Russian mob, which probably has to do with him being a weapons designer."

"Let's open the tequila, shall we?" Sa'Rhi suggested.

The next morning, someone knocked on the door, and Winterstorm looked through the little peephole.

"I believe we have some unwanted guests," Winterstorm announced.

When the door opened, a maid answered.

"Where's the person staying in this room?" a man asked.

"She went sightseeing for the day," she said in Russian.

After the men left, she stopped the illusion.

"Those men were from the Russian mob," Sa'Rhi said.

"I didn't know you can read minds too, Sa'Rhi!" she remarked.

"I can't, but I overheard one of them say the FSB was on their way up," Sa'Rhi said.

"Let's see what they have to say," she said.

They knocked on the door, and she answered.

"Why are you looking for Mr. Payson?" he asked.

"Someone abducted him, and I am here to retrieve him," she replied.

"He returned home five days ago," he said.

"That wasn't the Real Mr. Payson, but his body-double," she insisted.

"Then you need to come with me to FSB headquarters," he demanded.

After arriving at his headquarters, another agent confronted her.

"Why are you here in Russia?" he asked.

"As I told your other agent, to find the Real Mr. Payson," she replied.

"That means the Russian mob must have him," he said.

"Why would they have him?" she asked.

"He has been working on a Railgun prototype," he answered.

"Railgun?" she asked.

"It's a gun that uses electromagnetic energy to kill, not bullets," he explained.

"Then I must stop them from getting it," she stated.

She waved her hand in front of his face.

"Your men will take me back to the hotel, and we never had this conversation," she said.

They drove her back to her hotel.

"We need to find where they are holding Mr. Payson," she said.

"I saw two men watching us as we walked into the hotel," Sa'Rhi said.

She approached one of the men.

"Where are you holding Mr. Payson," she said.

"I don't know him," he insisted.

With a thought, she emitted that powerful pheromone.

"You smell so delicious," he said.

"You can have me for the information I need," she replied. "Where is Mr. Payson?"

"We are holding him at an old abandoned gulag, two hours away from Moscow," he said.

"Drive me there," she ordered.

They arrived at an old gulag camp.

"While I am looking for Mr. Payson, we will be in the back seat making love," she said.

She found Mr. Payson locked inside a cell.

"Who are you?" Mr. Payson asked.

"I was sent by Victoria to retrieve you," she answered.

When they got into the car, the man was smoking a cigarette.

"Time to drive me back to the hotel," she said.

He drove them back to Moscow, dropped them off, and returned to his post as though nothing had happened.

She and Mr. Payson boarded the next flight to San Francisco, and then to Sky Harbor Airport in Phoenix. As she parked across the street from her agency, she waved her hand in front of him.

"You two enjoyed Australia together, and just returned to Phoenix," she said.

She then went into his subconscious to remove any thoughts of a railgun. She considered such a weapon far too dangerous for anyone to have.

After she woke them, Victoria thanked her with a check for $50,000. As they drove home, Victoria called the police to have the imposter arrested.

"We've successfully solved another case, Winterstorm," Sa'Rhi said.

"We did, and we deserve a pint of chocolate ice cream," she replied.

Afterward, they enjoyed a few old Magnum P.I. Episodes, but after number four, they went to bed. When Winterstorm woke the next morning, she was looking at herself lying on the other side of her bed.

"Sa'Rhi, I think you better open your eyes," she said.

"Don't tell me it's time to get up already," Sa'Rhi said. "Wait… how can I be looking at you."

"I don't know, but we're two people now!" she said.

They hugged and then cried in each other's arms.

They began using their separate identities to their advantage.

When Winterstorm searched for clues inside houses to help her clients, Sa'Rhi would appear as her in public. It was a win-win situation as their clientele increased due to their high success rate. But, they also discovered that they had identical abilities, which they used when necessary.

One morning as Winterstorm drove to work, she spotted someone following her. When she made the next right turn, she saw that it was Wayne Hendricks. He became a private investigator after being terminated alongside Chief Dickens for gross incompetence.

"So, he wants to play games, does he?" she said.

She made another quick right turn, and after he made the same turn, she was gone.

After she arrived at work, she began reviewing case notes on one of her current investigations. A few minutes later, Summer Fox, Sa'Rhi's human alias, walked into the agency. In time, they discovered that they were able to transmute themselves into other people for short time-periods.

"Wayne Hendricks was following me this morning," Winterstorm said.

"So that's why he's watching the agency through binoculars," Sa'Rhi said.

Winterstorm got angry and went out the back way to confront him.

"Why are you following me," she yelled from his passenger window.

He jumped and nearly pissed his pants.

"I've been curious about your ninety-five percent success rate in solving cases when most of the private investigators, including myself, rarely get above seventy," he said.

"Instead of following me, why don't you just ask me?" she said.

"Because I didn't think you would give me an honest answer," he said.

"You're right," she yelled. "So, get the hell out of here."

He sped off as she returned to the agency.

"So, why is he snooping around?" Sa'Rhi asked.

"He's wondering why we're the most successful agency in Phoenix, which means we haven't seen the last of him," she said.

"There's one way to stop him," Sa'Rhi said.

Sa'Rhi explained her idea.

Winterstorm knew that Wayne would follow her as she put Sa'Rhi's plan into effect. As she drove out of town, she turned down a dirt road. He waited on the shoulder until she was out of sight, and then he followed her. A mile down the road, he saw her car at an old farmhouse, and he parked his behind a grove of trees. As he looked around, he saw an old barn in disrepair, a weather-beaten tool shed, and a small herd of llamas inside a fenced area. He carefully crept up to the house and peeked into a window. He saw Detective Winterstorm talking to someone, but when the other person appeared, it was her twin, and he gasped. Suddenly, the first Winterstorm vanished from his view.

"Why are you following me?" she asked angrily.

He nearly pissed himself again.

"Now, I understand why your success rate is so high, you have a twin sister," he said.

"I think you should come inside for an explanation," she said.

As he walked into the house, he sat on the middle chair because he somehow knew it was there for him. As Winterstorm sat down, she called Sa'Rhi into the room.

"You do have a twin sister?" he asked.

"Do you remember the jewelry store heist?" she asked.

"Yes, where Officer Penelope Wynterbourne handled three suspects all by herself," he stated.

"No, Wayne, that's not what happened at all," she said. "Because you didn't back me up, I was fatally shot by one of the suspects."

"There is no way in hell you could be Penelope Wynterbourne," he stated.

"But, I am, Wayne," she said.

"How?" he asked.

"After the suspect shot me, Sa'Rhi sent her thoughts into my mind," she said. "As I was about to die, she symbiotically joined with me, and then later, I took on her appearance, but for some unknown reason, we became two separate beings."

"What you're saying is science fiction mumbo jumbo, so this must be a joke to teach me a lesson," he said.

She changed back into Penelope right before his eyes.

"Oh, my God! It is you, but how is it possible?" he asked.

"You're right about teaching you a lesson, and we were going to give you a choice, but we decided to put you into one of those llamas outback," she said.

He laughed.

They focused their minds on him, and he vanished.

"I think he'd be more receptive this time," Sa'Rhi said.

They went outside to the llamas, called his name, and one of them walked up to them.

"I'm sorry, Penelope, change me back!" he asked.

"We're giving you thirty days to think about what you did," she said.

"Please, don't leave me like this!" he pleaded.

"See you in thirty days," she said.

They walked away.

"You don't think we're being too hard on him, do you," Winterstorm asked.

"He's getting his just desserts," Sa'Rhi said. "But we should be thankful to him."

"Why?" she asked.

"If it weren't for him, we wouldn't be together," Sa'Rhi said.

They hugged.

"What case are we working on today," Sa'Rhi asked.

"There's been a gang in Laveen demanding protection money from various mom and pop stores and restaurants," she said.

After they drove to Laveen, they entered Ricardo's Mexican Restaurant as Penelope Wynterbourne and Summer Fox, and the owners greeted them.

"How long has the gang been a problem?" Penelope asked.

"For six months, and their price keeps going up," Sylvia lamented.

"When are they returning?" Summer asked.

"This afternoon," Ricardo said. "That's why we hired you."

"I want you and your staff to take the day off," Penelope stated.

After everyone left, they changed back into Winterstorm and Sa'Rhi.

That afternoon, five gang members entered the restaurant as Winterstorm stood behind the register, and Sa'Rhi was sitting at the bar.

"I'm sorry, but we closed the restaurant due to a rat problem," Winterstorm said.

"We're here for our protection money," one of the men said.

Winterstorm and Sa'Rhi laughed.

"You five couldn't protect your mother from a brown paper bag," she said.

"What the fuck does that mean?" he asked.

He then saw Sa'Rhi.

"Are you fucking elves?" he asked.

"Whatever we are, you five are going down!" she stated.

The men laughed.

"I think you should get your whole gang together in here, and maybe you'll get lucky enough to take me down," she said.

"You insult us while you hide behind the register!" he yelled.

"Oh, I'm sorry! Is that holding you back," she said sarcastically. "I'll meet you right over there."

"You're going to pay for insulting us, bitch!" he yelled.

"You have no idea who you are messing with," Sa'Rhi said.

They then circled her and took out their knives.

"Now, we'll see wins this fight," he said.

Suddenly, the gang members were on the ground in pain without their knives.

"What the fuck just happened?" he yelled.

"Maybe, you should call in some backup!" she said.

He called his leader.

Thirty minutes later, the entire gang was inside the restaurant.

"Is this all of you?" she asked.

"Yeah, and we're all here to make sure you never give us another problem," he said.

"I'll give you one chance to turn yourselves in," she said.

"You're one fucking crazy bitch, aren't you?" he said.

"You have no idea," Winterstorm said, smiling.

"Are you fucking elves?" the leader asked.

"Why do you ask? Do you like our pointed ears?" Winterstorm asked.

As they talked, a group of cats wandered inside the restaurant.

"Friends of yours?" he asked.

"As I told your man, we have a rat problem, and the restaurant is closed, so they're here for dinner," she said.

"Are you calling us rats?" he asked.

"If the shoe fits," she said.

Suddenly, the cats turned into large Bengal Tigers and herded the gang into a corner.

"If you hand over all of your cash, we'll let you live," she said.

After they handed over nearly three thousand dollars, the tigers turned back into cats.

"For that you elven bitches, we're going to cut you into pieces and bury you in the desert," the leader said.

"I guess you didn't learn anything the first go around', so it's time to feed the cats," she said.

Suddenly, the gang turned into rats, and the cats chased them out.

Winterstorm and Sa'Rhi laughed.

"I think that was our best illusion ever!" Sa'Rhi said.

"Time to celebrate another job well done," she said.

Sa'Rhi grabbed a bottle of Jose Cuervo while Winterstorm sliced the limes, and poured salt into two small bowls. After three shots, two police officers walked into the restaurant.

"What the hell happened in here?" one of them asked. "Several witnesses say they saw rats running out of here with cats chasing after them, and then there were puffs of smoke, and the rats turned into the local gang running for their lives."

"Oh, those boys!" Winterstorm said. "They tried to collect protection money from us."

"Those we have caught thus far have confessed to several crimes in the area, and asked us to protect them from El Cuco by taking them directly to jail," he said.

"Why would adult men fear the boogeyman?" Sa'Rhi asked.

"No clue, Ma'am," he said.

After they left, Winterstorm called Ricardo to tell him that it was safe to return and that she left the money donated by the gang in his office.

Thirty days later, she and Sa'Rhi returned to see Wayne.

They called out his name, and he came over to them.

"What's it going to be Wayne," Winterstorm asked.

"I am truly sorry that I didn't back you up at the Jewelry store," he said sadly. "After you put me here, I had time to think about what I did and didn't do as a police officer, and that forced me to be honest with myself. I was a terrible police officer, and I understand why they fired me, so I'm not going to ask for your forgiveness."

"So, you decided to leave town?" she asked.

"No, because I found love, and I am asking for a favor," he said.

"What kind of favor?" she asked.

"Is there a place you can send us so we can live in peace," he asked.

"There's one thing we didn't tell you, Wayne," she said. "The llamas are not what they appear. They're elves from a mythical island called Hy-Brasil. To teach you a life lesson, they volunteered to help us because they owed us a favor."

"Did you say you found love?" Sa'Rhi asked.

"Yes, with Elaria," he said.

"Is this true Elaria," Sa'Rhi asked.

When she revealed herself, she was a tall, fair-skinned, red hair beauty with green emerald eyes.

"It's true, Princess Sa'Rhi, but I prefer to call him Ewan," Elaria said.

"It's rare when an elf finds love with a human, and that says something about you, Wayne," Sa'Rhi said. "Go stand next to your beloved."

They turned Wayne back into human form, and then he and Elaria held hands.

"Henceforth, Wayne Hendricks shall be known as Ewan of Hy-Brasil," Sa'Rhi said.

"You are fortunate to have someone like Elaria at your side," Winterstorm said.

As she and Sa'Rhi stood together, they sent them all back to Hy-Brasil.

Suddenly, two beams of light appeared.

"Winterstorm of Earth and Sa'Rhi of Ba'Kar, we send you salutations," a voice said.

"Who are you?" Winterstorm asked.

"We are the watchers of a galaxy known as Xenia on the opposite side of the universe," the voice said.

"What can we do for you?" Sa'Rhi asked.

"When you two were one, you found justice for victims, and as two, you showed forgiveness and compassion to those who have wronged you," the voice said.

"Are you the ones responsible for separating us?" Winterstorm asked.

"We are," the voice said.

"Why?" she asked.

"It was to test you," the voice said.

"For what reason?" Sa'Rhi asked.

"There is a planet in the Xenia Galaxy called Athernia with a humanoid population similar to Earth, and we, its watchers, want you as its rulers," the voice said.

"Why can't you rule over the planet?" Winterstorm asked.

"We are forbidden to interfere with the development of the planets in the Xenia Galaxy, no matter the outcome," the voice said.

"Wouldn't we hinder that development being from a different world?" Winterstorm asked.

"Although we can only observe the planet's development, we are allowed to choose its rulers," the voice said.

"Would we be free to rule as we see fit?" Sa'Rhi asked.

"We would not interfere with your sovereignty," the voice said.

"Would we be permitted to use our abilities if necessary," Winterstorm asked.

"Yes," the voice said.

"How long do you want us to rule there?" Sa'Rhi asked.

"You will leave what you know of Earth behind," the voice said.

"Are you saying that we'll rule Athernia for an indefinite period?" Winterstorm asked.

"If you accept our gift, and we take you there in a blink of an eye, a thousand of years on Earth would have passed," the voice said.

"In other words, it's a one-way trip for us?" Winterstorm said.

"It is, but the choice is yours," the voice said.

Winterstorm and Sa'Rhi had a long conversation as the Watchers waited.

"We may regret our decision later, but let's do it!" they said in unison.

The End

The Langston Twins Murder Mysteries

IN THE SMALL town of Crescent Grove, Iowa, it was a freezing day when the power grid went offline because of high demand. Afterward, dark billowing clouds formed over chimneys as the town's people waited for their power to return, but on this particular day, it didn't.

As night approached, candles, gas lanterns, and battery-powered lights were on in every household as families gathered to do what families did behind closed doors.

It was on this day that Delta Wayburn, Attorney at Law, decided to catch up on her casework. When she noticed the time, it was 7:00 p.m. Delta put the completed case files on Anna Goodwin's desk to file at the courthouse in the morning, and then she put the remaining ones in the in-basket. On her way to the Crescent Grove Cafe for some hot coffee and a slice of their delicious cherry pie, Delta slipped on an ice patch and hit her head on the sidewalk. She was dazed momentarily.

Hiding in the shadows of a building recess across the street was someone watching her. They received a text, telling them what to do next, and then they left.

After Delta sat up, she felt dampness on the back of her head. She picked herself off the ground and continued to her destination. When she walked into the bakery, Lisa Green greeted her.

"What happened, Delta you're bleeding," Lisa noted.

"I slipped on some ice and bumped my head," she said.

"Maybe, you should go to the emergency room," Lisa offered.

"I'll be okay, Lisa," she said.

"Are you sure?" Lisa asked.

"I'm sure," she said. "While I'm in the bathroom, I'll take my usual order."

She went to the restroom to wash the blood off her head. As she blotted it away with a wet paper towel, she felt a bump, and then she returned to her table.

Across town, the Langston Twins, Agatha, and Agnes, 60 years of age, were resting comfortably in their La-Z-Boy chairs, enjoying the warmth of their fireplace. They recently moved back to Crescent Grove because their husbands died in a freak accident on their way back from Winnipeg, Canada. As they waited for the signal to turn green, a logging truck driver wasn't paying attention to the light ahead, and he made a sudden stop beside them. The truck's load shifted, breaking the heavy chains holding the massive logs in place, and they flattened the SUV with their husbands inside.

When their husbands were alive, busy managing their multi-million-dollar companies, the sisters were well-renowned cold murder case consultants, but after their husband's demise, they decided to retire and live a quiet life.

"I think we should offer our expertise to the local police department," Agatha said.

"I think that's a splendid idea, Aggie," she said.

"Are you saying that you're bored like me?" Agatha asked.

"Yes, dear sister, quite bored with this so-called quiet life," she said.

After Delta finished her order, she felt slightly dizzy when she stood up, but she still managed to drive home. When she unlocked the front door and stepped inside, she could see her breath, realizing that a window was open somewhere inside, and then she caught a familiar scent in the air. As she tried to walk back out, someone hit her from behind. They took most of her money from her wallet, leaving two twenties behind, disregarding the Rolex Watch on her wrist. They locked the front door, and then they exited the same way they came in. Once outside, they relocked the window, and then pushed the glass pane they removed back into place, resealed it, and then rubbed dirt into it in an attempt to hide their deed.

The next morning Anna Goodwin filed the paperwork on her desk at the courthouse. When she returned to the office, Delta wasn't at her desk.

After the Langston sisters arrived at the police department, they asked to speak to the new chief of police. The deputy took them to Walter Mayhew's office, and they waited.

"We found him!" Agnes pointed.

They both laughed because the placard read Walter "Waldo" Mayhew. He returned to his office.

"How may I help you?" he asked.

"We're the Langston Sisters, and we came to offer our services," Agatha said.

"Like janitorial services?" he asked rudely.

"No, we came to offer you our murder expertise," Agnes said defensively.

"This department doesn't need nor want your services," he said rudely.

Suddenly his phone rang.

"Dead? How?" he asked. "I'll be there in a few minutes!"

"Who's dead?" Agnes asked.

"That's police business!" he said sternly.

They waited for the chief outside so they could follow him.

"I wonder what happened!" Agnes asked.

"I'm sure we can talk to our old friend, Doc Miller, to find out," Agatha said.

Three days later, as Delta's funeral was underway, they went to visit Dr. Miller.

"What brings you two around here?" he asked.

"We're inquiring about Delta Wayburn's death," Agnes said.

"She slipped on an ice patch and hit her head on the sidewalk after leaving her office. Lisa Green told the new chief of police after she heard about Delta's death. Lisa told him about the blood on her head," he said.

"Who found the body?" Agnes asked.

"Anna Goodwin, because she was worried about Delta not being in her office," he said.

"Was there anything strange found at the scene?" Agatha asked.

"According to Lieutenant Daniels, there were two things. She was facing the front door with an outstretched arm, and one of her shoes were missing," he said.

"What did the new chief say about her death," Agnes said.

"He called it an accident," he said.

"What do you think?" Agatha asked.

"After I took x-rays, and then examined the back of her head, I found some inconsistencies with her injuries," he said.

"What kind of inconsistencies?" Agnes asked.

"When I examined the location where she fell, it didn't match her injury, and I noted that in my report," he said.

"What about the missing shoe?" Agnes asked.

"Lieutenant Daniels said he couldn't find it," he said.

"Were there any open windows in the house?" Agatha asked.

"Everything was locked," he said.

"Were any other items missing?" Agnes asked.

"According to Anna Goodwin, everything was in its proper place," he said.

"Could she have been murdered?" Agnes asked.

"Maybe, but how did her killer leave since Delta had the only set of keys," he said.

"That's a real poser, isn't it?" Agatha said.

"I think it's time we talk to our old friend Mayor Hobson," Agnes said. "It seems odd that the chief of police was in such a hurry to close the case."

As they walked to their car, they discussed the case.

"Before we talk to Gene, I think we need to investigate the new police chief," Agatha said.

"Agreed, because he gave off an odd vibe," Agnes said.

After contacting his last employer, who sent them a copy of his personnel file, they noted that he had multiple disciplinary actions against him, and they printed everything.

"Agatha and Agnes, it's so nice to see you again," Mayor Hobson said.

"It's been a while, hasn't it?" Agatha asked.

"Nearly thirty-five years," he said. "So, why did you want to see me?"

"We investigated the new chief of police, and in his personnel file from his last employer, he's had multiple disciplinary actions for closing cases without conducting proper investigations; Internal Affairs investigated him twice for criminal misconduct, and four of his evaluations ranged from being incompetent to grossly incompetent. So, we're wondering how he got hired?" Agatha asked.

"What evidence do you have to support those accusations?" he asked.

They laid a folder onto his desk, and he flipped through it. He then made a call.

"Why didn't you do a background check?" he asked.

"It wasn't in the budget," the voice said.

"I want him gone by the end of the day; do you hear me!" he yelled.

"So, what brought on the need to investigate him?" he asked.

"He closed the case on Delta Wayburn's death much too quickly, ignoring Dr. Miller's observations, as well as other evidence that alluded to a different conclusion. We think someone murdered her," Agnes said.

"Murdered?" he asked.

"Where she hit her head on the ice didn't match Dr. Miller's findings; she was missing a shoe which the police couldn't find; and when Anna Goodwin and the police found her body, she was facing the front door with an outstretched hand. We think she was trying to leave when someone hit her from behind," Agatha said.

"What would you like me to do?" he asked.

"Make us Crescent Grove Police Consultants," Agnes said.

"What will that cost the city?" he asked.

"Absolutely nothing," Agatha said.

"I will do as you request under one condition," he said. "That you two have dinner with me this evening to catch up."

"Agreed," Agatha said.

He called his secretary to bring in the Bible. He swore them in as the newly appointed police consultants. From there, they returned to the police department.

"What are you two doing here?" Chief Mayhew asked.

"We came to review the case file for Delta Wayburn's death," Agnes asked.

"As I told you before, this department doesn't need nor want your help," he said.

"Sorry to tell you, but we now work for the city as police consultants," Agatha said.

"Police consultants?" he groaned.

"Have you finished packing yet?" Agatha asked rudely.

"Did you two have something to do with my termination?" he asked angrily.

"The only thing we did was provide the mayor with your police personnel file, which was quite an interesting read," Agnes said.

"How did you get my police personnel file?" he asked.

"Before we moved back here, we were nationally known police consultants, and we have access to whatever we need. You see, no one likes a bad cop, and your last employer gladly gave you up," Agatha said.

"Here's one last question for you," Agnes asked.

"What?" he yelled.

"Where's Waldo now?" Agnes said.

Agatha and Agnes laughed as he stormed out of the building.

"Are you Agatha and Agnes?" Lieutenant Tommy Daniels asked.

"We are," Agatha said.

"I brought you Delta Wayburn's case file," he said. "I guess, for now, I'm the acting police chief, and whatever you need, just ask."

"Thank you," Agnes said.

"By the way, if you two need space, we have an empty room with a table and two chairs that you could use," he said.

"We went to high school with Jason Daniels, are you related?" Agatha asked.

"He was my father?" he asked.

"What happened to him?" Agatha asked.

"He died from pancreatic cancer two years ago," he said.

"I'm sorry, he was a good man," Agnes said. "Where is that room you were talking about?"

"I'll show you," he said.

He took them to the empty room, and then he returned to his duties.

"This room has possibilities," Agatha stated.

When they reviewed Delta's case file, they could quickly tell that Chief Mayhew did very little investigative work.

"I guess we can rule out robbery as a motive," Agnes suggested.

"What about the missing shoe?" Agatha asked.

"That's an odd piece of evidence, but maybe it was taken as a trophy," Agnes said.

"That would imply a serial killer," Agatha said.

"You're right, and a serial killer would have left evidence to showcase their work, so we can rule that one out as well," Agnes said.

"I think we should talk to Lisa Green," Agatha said.

They walked down the street to talk to Lisa. They each ordered coffee, and then Agatha told Lisa that they needed to interview her. Lisa brought their coffee and sat across from them.

"Why do you need to interview me?" Lisa asked.

"We had the mayor appoint us as police consultants so that we can investigate Delta Wayburn's murder," Agnes said.

"But, Chief Mayhew said it was an accident!" she said.

"He didn't do a proper investigation. As we reviewed Delta's case file, he ignored Dr. Miller's findings and other evidence, and we have reopened the investigation," Agatha said.

"I felt sad because I thought I should have done more after she hit her head," she said.

"The first injury wasn't serious, it was the blunt force trauma that killed her," Agatha said.

"What do you need to know?" she asked.

"Did Delta appear nervous or jumpy that night?" Agatha asked.

"She was her usual stubborn self, but she did make me worry because she always carried a lot of cash with her," she said.

"How much?" Agnes asked.

"When she paid at the register, I saw several hundred-dollar bills in her wallet," she said.

"When they found her body, the police, and then we ruled out burglary because she had forty dollars in her wallet, an untouched Rolex Watch on her wrist and nothing was missing from the house," Agatha said.

"That's very odd, isn't it," she said.

"Thank you for your help, but we must visit Anna Goodwin now," Agnes said.

They left the cafe and walked to Delta's legal practice.

"We need to talk to you about Delta Wayburn," Agatha said.

"What about her?" Anna asked.

"The mayor has appointed us as police consultants, and we're investigating her murder," Agnes said.

"Murder?" she asked. "Chief Mayhew said it was an accident."

"Whoever killed Delta left only forty dollars in her wallet to cover for their theft, left her Rolex Watch untouched, and took nothing from the house except her shoe," Agatha said.

"On the day of her murder, she had a thousand dollars in her wallet, so the thief took over nine hundred dollars from her wallet," she said.

"That confirms what Lisa Green told us, supporting our theory that someone killed Delta for another reason," Agnes said.

"How do you explain the missing shoe?" she asked.

"The one piece of evidence we can't explain," Agatha said.

"What happens to her legal practice?" Agnes asked.

"A new attorney is coming to take over her caseload, but he already has a paralegal, so I'll be out of a job and unable to finish my law degree," she said.

"How would you like to work for us," Agnes asked.

"What would I have to do?" she asked.

"The same job you're doing except for more research," Agatha said.

"Would I still be able to attend classes?" she asked.

"Of course, and we'll pay you the same salary," Agnes offered.

"When do I start?" she asked.

"You already have," Agatha said.

"How long has Delta had her practice here?" Agnes asked.

"About six months," she said.

"What kind of legal work did she do before she came here?" Agatha asked.

"She worked as a malpractice attorney for an insurance company," she said.

"That's a good place to start our investigation!" Agnes said.

"She kept her case summaries on a USB drive if she needed to refer to them," she said.

"Please look through them to see if anything sticks out," Agnes said.

"Do you have the keys to Delta's house?" Agatha asked.

"Yes, I'll get them for you," she said.

As Anna looked through Delta's case summaries, Agatha and Agnes drove to Delta's house to find the murder weapon. As they walked inside, a holiday snow globe immediately caught Agatha's eye.

"Agnes, do you still have that small bottle of luminol with you?" Agatha asked.

"I do," Agnes replied.

Agnes picked up the snow globe with gloved hands and sprayed it. A few moments later, traces of blood appeared. They called Lieutenant Daniels.

Ten minutes later, he arrived.

"You found the murder weapon," he said.

"We did, but what doesn't make sense is how Chief Mayhew missed an obvious clue," Agnes said.

"We need to determine how the killer got into the house," Agatha said.

"While you're doing that, I'll take the snow globe to Dr. Miller for analysis," he said.

They examined the doors, but there was no evidence of tampering. They then considered the upstairs windows, but there was no evidence that someone used a ladder. As they examined each window on the outside, Agnes noted a windowpane with excess dirt on the sealant. She grabbed a paperclip from her purse and pushed the sharp end into the sealant. Instead of being rubbery as it should have been, it went straight in. She called Agatha.

"What did you find?" Agatha asked.

"This is where the killer entered and exited the house," Agnes said. "We better call Lieutenant Daniels."

A few minutes later, he arrived, and they showed him what they found. He then confided in them, and they had a lengthy conversation.

"As Dr. Miller examined the snow globe, he found blood, but all the fingerprints had been wiped clean," he said.

"Whoever Killed Delta knew what they were doing," Agatha surmised.

Agatha's cell phone rang.

"Hello," Agatha said.

"Hi, Agatha," Anna said. "I think I found something."

"We'll be there in a few minutes," Agatha said.

"What is it?" Agnes asked.

"Anna thinks she found something," Agatha said.

A few minutes later, they arrived at Delta's legal practice.

"What did you find?" Agatha asked.

"I printed a copy for you, and it gave me quite a stir. I had to read it three times to confirm what I was seeing," she said.

As they read the case summary, they noted that a doctor performed the wrong surgery on a female patient. He amputated her leg when she was in the hospital for a hysterectomy. There was a mix-up at the hospital because two women had the same last name. The woman sued the hospital, but the insurance company wouldn't pay the claim based on Delta Wayburn's recommendations.

"That could explain the missing shoe, but who killed her?" Agatha asked.

"Keep reading," Anna said.

As they continued reading, her son was Walter Mayhew.

"Now, it makes perfect sense why he did a shoddy investigation," Agnes said.

Agnes called Lieutenant Daniels and told them who they thought was Delta's killer. He issued an APB out on Walter Mayhew.

Walter Mayhew was arrested in Des Moines, Iowa, two weeks later. Agatha and Agnes went to interview him.

"I gave my confession to the District Attorney, what else do you want?" he asked.

"To ask you a curious question. Why did you take Delta's shoe, and the money from her wallet?" Agatha asked.

"What are you talking about?" he asked.

"Anna Goodwin and Lisa Green confirmed that on the day Delta Wayburn was murdered, she had a substantial amount of cash in her purse, and Dr. Miller told us about the missing shoe," Agnes said.

"I don't know anything about missing money, but when I saw

Delta's body, she had both shoes on her feet," he said. "Who told Dr. Miller that one of her shoes was missing?"

"Lieutenant Daniels," Agatha said.

"Maybe, you should ask him about the shoe," he said.

Suddenly, his face went pale, and his head hit the table. They called for help, but when help arrived, he was dead. They requested an immediate tox screen on his blood.

The next day, they received a call from the Des Moines Medical Examiner. He then told them that Walter Mayhew died from Fentanyl poisoning.

"I don't think Walter Mayhew killed Delta, and yet he confessed to the crime," Agatha said.

"But, the question is 'Why?'" Agnes said.

"Maybe someone threatened him or his mother's life," Agatha said.

"I wonder if he had visitors while he was in jail," Agatha said.

"Let's find out," Agatha said.

They learned that he had only one visitor, an Attorney named Cynthia Payne. They went online to research her, but she doesn't exist.

They went to see the mayor.

"What's going on?" Gene asked.

"We received a call confirming that someone murdered Walter Mayhew," Agnes said.

"Murdered? How?" he asked.

"Someone poisoned him with Fentanyl, and the only visitor he had was an attorney named Cynthia Payne, who doesn't exist, but we came to ask you about Tommy Daniels."

"What about him?" he asked.

"How long have you known him?" Agnes asked.

"He applied five months ago for his current position after Delta Wayburn arrived," he said. "I hired him because his father Jason Daniels was a good police officer, and so far he hasn't disappointed me. But, before then, the last time I saw Tommy was when he was six years old. After Jason Daniels and his wife divorced, they moved to Johnston, Iowa."

"We believe that Walter Mayhew didn't kill Delta Wayburn, and both of their murders are somehow connected," Agatha said.

"If that's true, please be careful," he said.

"We will," Agnes said.

After they drove home, Anna Goodwin came to see them.

"Would you like some tea, Anna," Agatha asked.

"Sounds great," she said.

"We need to take a closer look into Delta and Walter's deaths," Agnes said.

"Do you think they are connected?" Anna asked.

"Yes, and the one variable they have in common is the insurance company called Universal Medical Malpractice Affiliates, who employed Delta," Agnes said.

"But, we need to proceed with caution," Agatha said. "I believe they're watching us."

"Why do you think that?" Anna asked.

"We don't think Officer Tommy Daniels is the real Tommy Daniels," Agnes said.

"There is a way to check without him finding out," Anna asked.

"How?" Agatha asked.

"By using Classmates.com," Anna said.

"We've never heard of it?" Agnes asked.

"If he ever had school pictures taken, we can find him online," Anna said. "Do you know where he lived or what year he graduated from high school?"

"No clue, but we can approximate the time he graduated from the police academy in Johnston, Iowa," Agnes said.

"Where's your computer?" Anna asked.

They took her to their war room as they called it.

Anna was surprised by all of their technology and computers in one room.

"Why do you have all of this technology?" Anna asked.

"Before our husbands died, we were cold case consultants," Agnes said proudly. "You can use any computer in here that you like."

It took Anna all of five minutes to find him.

"Is this him?" Anna asked.

"No, which means we have a problem," Agnes said.

"Can you look at the Obits in Johnston, Iowa, I have a hunch," Agatha said.

They discovered that the real Tommy Daniels and his mother died in a recent car accident.

"Someone must have killed them like the others," Agatha said.

"We need to look inside Delta's house. I believe what we need to put all of this together is hidden there," Agnes said. "But, first, we need to stop by the recorder's office to get the building plans for her house."

They arrived at the recorder's Officer a few minutes before they closed. After they got a copy of Delta's house plans, they drove to her house. When they went inside, they rolled out the plans on the kitchen table to compare the size of each room. They found a small hidden space and then proceeded to the master bedroom. Inside the walk-in closet, they discovered a lever hidden beneath a pair of Delta's shoes. When they pulled on the bar, a panel slid open.

"I don't believe it!" Anna said.

"I wonder, what's inside?" Agatha asked.

"There's only one way to find out," Agnes said.

After using a cell phone for a flashlight, they found a small light switch inside, where they found a file cabinet. Agatha and Agnes removed the files and placed them on Delta's bed.

Lieutenant Daniels suddenly walked into the room.

"Thank you," he said with his gun out.

"Are you going to kill us?" Agatha asked

"Sorry, ladies," he said, putting his gun back into its holster. "I'm Special Agent Walker with the FBI."

"FBI?" Agnes asked.

We knew you weren't Tommy Daniels because we discovered that he and his mother died in a car accident," Agatha said.

"I had a fellow agent working with me named Linda Carlisle, who resembled Delta, who was an attorney before joining the FBI, and an assassin killed her. We have the real Delta Wayburn in custody," he said.

"Why all the murders?" Agnes said.

"Universal Medical Malpractice Affiliates is a drug money laundering operation. If there were an actual claim, they would threaten claimants with death to silence them," he said. "When there was an actual payout, it was paid to someone working for them."

"That means you suspect someone here in Crescent Grove," Agnes said.

"It's Mayor Hobson," he said.

"Why would he be mixed up in all of this?" Agnes asked.

"That's a good question, Agnes," Mayor Hobson said with a gun pointed at them.

Agent Walker tried to draw his weapon, but the mayor shot him.

"Why are you mixed up in all of this, Gene?" Agatha asked.

"I was tired of barely making ends meet when someone made me an offer I couldn't pass up," he said. "My job was simple. All I had to do was to act the part of a medical malpractice claimant, and as my reward, I have over two million dollars in a Cayman Islands account."

"Why did you kill Delta Wayburn?" Agnes asked.

"I didn't kill anyone," he said. "The assassin who killed Delta and Walter is standing beside you."

"You played us like a violin, Anna," Agnes said.

"What kind of an assassin would I be if I couldn't put one past the most famous murder consultants in the world," Anna said.

"Bravo," Agnes said. "I want to thank you two for playing your parts so predictably well."

"What do you mean?" Anna asked.

"We knew you weren't Anna Goodwin or Cynthia Payne because neither of you exists, but sadly we were too late to save Walter; we also knew that Gene was involved when Agent Walker revealed himself to us before Walter's arrest; when we visited Gene a second time, we knew about his gun, and we replaced his bullets with blanks; Nancy and Tommy are still among the living, we just killed them off for your benefit to blow Agent Walker's cover, which was part of the plan; We also found the small space in Delta's closet when we investigated how you got into her house. We turned over the files we found to the FBI. Those on the bed are fake," Agatha said.

"Come on in boys," Agnes said.

Several police officers hiding inside the house came into the room to arrest Gene and the assassin. Agent Walker got off the floor.

"Before they take me away, what about the missing shoe?" the assassin asked.

"There was never a missing shoe. When Agent Carlisle slipped on the night you murdered her, Lisa Green told us that she was limping because of the fall, but that's not why she had a limp. You see, during her fall, she broke one of her heels on her shoes. Agent Carlisle was angry when she got home and kicked the shoe into the bushes before she walked into the house," Agatha said.

The assassin laughed as they escorted her out.

"Thank you, Agatha and Agnes; we couldn't have done it without you," he said.

"We're sorry about Agent Carlisle," Agatha said.

"Sadly, it's part of the job," he said.

"If you like, we could be FBI consultants?" Agnes said.

"I just happen to have two badges with your names on them," he said.

"You're a sneaky one, Agent Walker," Agatha said.

A few months later, two men, Stan Wilcox and Joey Hargrove sat in a booth at Kelsey's bar in San Diego, drowning their sorrows, one shot after another. After learning about their death sentences, as they called them, they met one another at a group therapy session for the terminally ill, and since their lives were hauntingly similar, they bonded. Instead of continuing with the group, they decided to adopt a daily ritual of drowning themselves in alcohol. As they downed each shot, they bitterly complained about being nobodies in a somebody world.

After several shots of Vodka, they discussed what they wanted to do on their bucket lists, but for them, it was idle chatter to pass the time. Besides being nobodies, they were do-nothings. A woman sitting in a dark booth overheard their sad lamentations, making her smile. She scribbled down a number on a napkin, dropped it between the two men, and vanished into the night.

Johnny Star, the lead singer of the Heavy Metal Band Netherland, did his usual lines of Cocaine before performing on stage. As the band began to play, he missed his cue, but this wasn't unusual for him because he's done it before. The Band Manager, Neal Smith, went to check on him. When he walked into Johnny's dressing room, he was dead, and he found a note *'After the affair at the victory ball, I had an appointment with death.'*

He called the police, but they were baffled by the cryptic message Johnny left behind. An autopsy revealed that he died from an overdose of Digitoxin, which he took for an irregular heartbeat caused by years of Cocaine use.

Roger Horner, a high-profile federal prosecutor, who in his earlier career, served as a defense attorney, received a box of Mon Cheri Liquor Chocolates from a grateful client. As he worked throughout the day, he had sampled over half of the thirty brandy and cherry-filled delights. As he stood from his desk, he suddenly fell to the floor and died. Later, a note was found on his office desk *'A dumb witness caused peril at the end house.'* This time, the police called the FBI.

Agent Walker flew Agatha and Agnes to San Diego to consult, and he met them outside the terminal.

"We are very disappointed. Agatha said," she said.

"What happened?" he asked.

"The only thing we got on our flight was peanuts, and we're famished," Agnes said.

"Then dinner is on me," he said, smiling.

They stopped at an Olive Garden on his way to their hotel. Agatha and Agnes ordered Fettuccine Alfredo and Agent Walker, Lasagna. When the meal arrived, he took out the note found in Roger Horner's office.

"Sorry, but we don't discuss cases on an empty stomach," Agnes said admonishingly.

"I apologize," he said.

After dinner and two glasses of wine, Agatha asked to see the note.

"This is interesting!" Agatha said, handing it to Agnes.

"You're right, Aggie. Death by Agatha Christie," Agnes said.

"What are you talking about?" he asked.

"Were there any other recent deaths with a similar note?" Agatha asked.

"There was an odd suicide note Johnny Star left behind," he said.

"Can we see it?" Agnes asked.

"Let me call the investigating officer," he said.

He sent the note to Agent Walker's email. When he opened it, he showed it to Agatha and Agnes.

"Someone murdered Johnny Star," Agnes said.

"How did you come to that conclusion without looking at the crime scene," he asked.

"*The Affair at the Victory Ball* and *Appointment with Death* are Agatha Christie novels featuring Detective Hercule Poirot," Agatha said. "In the first novel, the victim died from a cocaine overdose, and in the second, the victim died from Digitoxin poisoning."

"In the first note, two Agatha Christie novels are mentioned. In *Dumb Witness*, the victim died from arsenic poisoning, and in *Peril at End House*, the victim died from a box of poisoned chocolates. They also featured Detective Hercule Poirot," Agnes said.

"Why him?" he asked.

"He was more of an armchair detective because he was short, overweight, and older in her books. He solved most of his cases through interviews and sometimes overheard conversations, a quick view of the murder scene, and then he was able to put it all together. Our methodology is similar because we solved cold case murders in the comfort of our home," Agatha said.

"Are you saying someone is challenging you two?" Agnes asked.

"I do," Agatha said.

"Why?" he asked.

"In the detective world, there is a division of who would be the better detective, Hercule Poirot or Sherlock Holmes," Agnes said.

"So, whoever is challenging you is a fan of Sherlock Holmes?" he asked.

"Maybe, but to find our killer, we need to determine how Johnny Star and Roger Horner are connected," Agatha said.

"Are you sure their deaths are connected?" he asked.

"Quite sure," Agnes said.

Stan and Joey received verbal instructions via the payphone outside Kelsey's Bar for their next task as their mysterious benefactor sat two tables away from Agent Walker, Agatha, and Agnes watching them. As she stared at Agatha and Agnes, she finally caught their eye, and they looked at her.

"Do you remember the blonde lady sitting in Lisa Green's bakery, and then the redhead that bumped into me at the airport?" Agatha asked.

"Yes, I remember them," Agnes said.

"She wants to say hello," Agatha said.

Agatha and Agnes raised their glasses in recognition of her diabolical deeds, and she raised hers as well.

"Who is that?" Agent Walker asked.

"Our killer and nemesis," Agnes said.

"Then I should arrest her!" he said.

"You'd be wasting your time because she has all the bases covered," Agatha said. "Just smile and raise your glass."

Afterward, the woman called the server over to her table to pay for their meal. The woman left the restaurant with a crooked smile.

"I don't believe we're dealing with a Sherlock Holmes fan, but rather a fan of Professor James Moriarty," Agatha said.

"Are you saying that she's that intelligent?" he asked.

"Yes, and she'll continue her murder spree to whatever end she has in mind," Agnes said.

"Then we should have stopped her!" he growled.

"She would be back on the streets within hours, so we need to find the link between Johnny Star and Roger Horner," Agatha said.

After leaving the restaurant, they went to Roger Horner's office to look at his old case files. Three hours later, they found the connection. After a woman gave birth to a baby girl, she accused Johnny Star of rape, but in a sworn court deposition, Roger Horner made her appear as a sex-starved groupie, who hung around the band. As a result, Roger Horner, who represented Johnny Star, asked to have the case dismissed. The Prosecuting Attorney, David Cross, and presiding Judge, Calvin Myers, agreed. Later on, the woman committed suicide. The baby girl became a ward of the state, and then she was adopted.

"I believe the adopted girl was the woman at Olive Garden," Agatha said.

"So, revenge must be her motive," Agnes said.

"Who do you think her next targets will be?" he asked.

"Judge Calvin Myers and David Cross," Agatha said.

"Then we must warn them," he said.

He was able to get in contact with Mr. Cross, but Judge Myers was out on the golf course, and he didn't have his phone with him. They sped to the Grand Golf Course only to find Judge Myers had been shot dead, and next to him was a note *'Since the cards are on the table, and there was murder on the links, there is one more to kill so the big four can rest in peace.'*

"It's too late for the judge, but we can still save Mr. Cross," Agnes said.

They sped to Mr. Cross's locale. As they walked into his office, he was about to use his nasal spray.

"Don't use it, or you'll die!" Agatha yelled.

"Who the hell are you?" Mr. Cross asked.

"We're the ones who warned you," Agnes said.

He put the nasal spray down.

"You think someone poisoned my nasal spray?" he asked.

"There is one sure way to find out," Agent Walker said.

He sprayed it on a plant, and it suddenly wilted.

"Oh my God!" he said. "How did you know?"

The woman orchestrating the murders is using Agatha Christie novels as clues in the notes her men leave behind," Agnes said.

"Who wants me dead?" he asked.

"Do you remember the Johnny Star rape case?" Agent Walker said.

"That was a very long time ago," he said.

"The woman had a child, and we believe that she is getting revenge for her mother's death," Agatha said.

"What about Judge Myers?" he asked.

"Dead like Johnny Star and Roger Horner," Agent Walker said.

"I should thank you for saving my life," he said.

As he stood by an open window, he felt a mosquito bite his neck.

"I hate this time of year because of all the mosquitos!" he said.

A moment later, he collapsed on the floor and died.

"What happened?" Agent Walker asked.

"The nose spray was a clever diversion," Agatha said.

His phone rang, and Agnes answered it.

"Sometimes, there is *Death in the clouds*," the woman said. "The showdown between us is tomorrow at midnight in the medical examiner's building, and you two must come alone."

The woman hung up.

"Who was that?" Agent Walker asked.

"It was her, using '*Death in the Clouds*,' as a clue," Agnes said. "She wants us to meet her tomorrow at midnight in the medical examiner's building alone."

"There is no way in hell that I will allow you to go in there alone!" he stated.

"If we don't meet with her, she'll find another way to end us," Agatha said. "It's a risk we must take, and if you like, we can wear wires. So, if there's any trouble, you can send in reinforcements."

"If I allow you to do such an insane thing, you will go in wearing bulletproof vests beneath your clothing," he said.

"Agreed," Agnes said.

After answering a lot of police questions, Agent Walker took them to their hotel.

Two hours later, Stan and Joey boarded the small plane destined for Maui because their benefactor told them it was a bonus for doing their job well. As the pilot introduced herself, Stan and Joey noted her good looks. She winked and told them to see what happens at 5,000 feet.

"It looks like we're going to be members of the mile-high club," Joey said.

The Cessna took off and was cruising at five thousand feet when the pilot put the plane on autopilot. When the pilot left the cockpit, Joey and Stan were excited until they saw that she was wearing a parachute. She said good luck boys and jumped out of the plane.

An hour later, the plane crashed near the beach.

The next morning, Agatha and Agnes were enjoying a continental breakfast. Agnes was reading the San Diego Union-Tribune when a story caught her eye.

"I know what happens to our nemesis's henchmen," Agatha said.

"I didn't know you were a psychic," Agnes said.

Agatha laughed.

"Our nemesis killed them yesterday," Agnes said.

"What are you talking about, Aggie?" Agnes asked.

She showed Agnes the article.

"I guess she's tying up loose ends, and unfortunately, her last clue had a double meaning, leaving just us to stop her," Agnes said.

Agent Walker sat at their table.

"Did you sleep well?" he asked.

"We were both a bit restless, but we're fine," Agnes said.

"Are you ready for tonight?" he asked.

"We are, but you don't have to worry about her henchmen being there," Agatha said.

"Why?" he asked.

"She killed them yesterday," Agnes said.

He read the article.

"So, you think this was her?" he asked.

"Yes," Agatha said. "At the meeting tonight, it will just be her and us, which was her plan all along, but we don't know why?" Agatha said.

Imaginative Tales

"Could it be about one of those cold murder cases you handled?" he asked.

"Possibly," Agnes said.

"I just remembered something, Agnes!" Agatha said. "Do you remember the case of the woman's body under the train trestle bridge?"

"Isn't that the case we thought was a suicide, and we passed on it?" Agnes said.

"It is, and I am wondering if our nemesis is the daughter she left behind?" Agatha said.

"Considering the facts, you may be right," Agnes said.

"Do you think Johnny Star killed her?" he asked.

"It wouldn't make sense to kill her after the judge dismissed the case," Agatha said.

"There are two sides to every story," Agnes said. "Is it possible to look through Mr. Cross's case files?"

They returned to David Cross's office. As Agatha and Agnes searched through his old case files, Agent Walker searched his desk when he found an envelope with *'In case of my death'* written on it. When Agent Walker read the letter, it was an admission of guilt for accepting a bribe from the Netherland Band Manager, Neal Smith, for twenty thousand dollars to have the rape case dismissed against Johnny Star. He also bribed Judge Myers.

"Netherland's Manager, Neal Smith, was worried about Johnny Star's case, and he bribed Judge Myers and Prosecuting Attorney David Cross to dismiss the case against him. I think that Neal Smith may have killed the woman to silence her," he said.

He then called an FBI Forensic Accountant.

"Could Neal Smith be in danger," Agatha asked.

"I don't think she knows about him," Agnes said.

Agent Walker received a call from the accountant, who confirmed that both men had deposited twenty thousand dollars into their bank accounts. He then called the police to have Neal Smith picked up for questioning.

"I think we should rest before tonight's festivities," Agnes said.

Agent Walker dropped them off at their hotel, while he went to question Neal Smith. After two hours of interrogation, he finally told Agent Walker that the woman was standing near the train trestle bridge when he tried to offer her money for her silence. She started walking away from him when she fell to her death. The police booked him for bribery and involuntary manslaughter. Agent Walker called Agatha and Agnes about the news.

It was 11:55 p.m. when Agatha and Agnes walked into the medical examiner's building alone. It was dark, and they used their cell phones as flashlights. Suddenly, a female voice spoke over the intercom.

"Take the elevator to the top floor," she said.

When they reached the top floor, the voice spoke again.

"Now go to room 425, and I will be waiting for you," she said.

As they approached room 425, the door opened, and she beckoned them inside.

"Are you aware that new evidence has surfaced depicting your mother's death as a tragic accident?" Agnes asked.

"What new information?" she asked.

"The FBI has the man in custody responsible for her death," Agnes said.

"How did she die?" she asked.

"Neal Smith bribed Judge Myers and the Prosecuting Attorney David Cross to have her rape case against Johnny Star dropped. On the night of her death, he was trying to offer her money to drop the case. When she backed away from him, she fell to her death," Agnes said.

"So, it was Neal Smith, Netherland's Manager, who set all of this into motion," she said. Since you two are wearing wires, I'm not going to say anything, so come on in boys."

"How did you know we were wearing wires?" Agnes asked.

She held up a hand-held device.

The FBI came in and arrested her.

"I will see you soon to finish our conversation," she said.

They took her away, as Agent Walker came into the room.

"She would give Professor Moriarty a run for his money," Agatha said thoughtfully.

"Without evidence linking her to the four murders, she will be back on the streets by tomorrow morning," he said.

"I think it's time we return to the hotel," Agnes said.

The next morning, the woman arrested by the FBI got her one phone call. Afterward, gas seeped into the FBI building, knocking everyone unconscious. When everyone awoke, Neal Smith was dead. Someone hanged him in his cell. Agent Walker called Agatha and Agnes.

"She played us like a violin," Agnes said.

"And got herself arrested," Agatha said.

"Agent Walker said that she was found unconscious in her cell," Agnes said.

"Damn, she's good," Agatha said. "The perfect crime and the perfect alibi."

"Thank you for that lovely compliment," she said. "Now, back to our conversation."

Agatha and Agnes were shocked.

"The looks on your faces are priceless," she said.

"How did you get our room?" Agatha asked.

"I used the maid's key, of course," she said. "You should always use both locks on the door to keep out intruders. I just came to say thank you for finding the truth. I was angry at you, but I can understand the reason you passed on my mother's case. So, I believe it's time for me to join her, but before I go, I will leave you one last Agatha Christie clue *'the curtain is closed.'*

After she ingested poison, Agent Walker ran into the room.

"What happened?" he asked.

"She thanked us for finding the truth about her mother's death, and then she drank a vial of poison," Agatha said.

"The case is now officially closed, and I'll be flying you back home tomorrow morning, but tonight dinner is on me."

A few days later, someone rang their doorbell. Agatha went to see who was at the door and found a box from FEDX. As she opened it, she found the entire Agatha Christie collection, and she called Agnes.

"What is it, Aggie?" she asked.

"She's alive!" Agatha said, pointing.

The End